Arithmophobia

by

Ruschelle Dillon

Mystery and Horror, LLC
Clearwater, FL

Arithmophobia

ISBN-13: 978-0-9981132-7-2

Arithmophobia

Dedication

To my Mom, Dad and husband. Thank you for your ardent support. I love you.

To my friends who show up in this book...and many of my other stories, thank you for your 'fandom' and friendships.

And a special thanks to John (Coconut), who believed in me and the monsters I've kept under my bed. Thank you for helping me feed them...

Table of Contents

Foreword

The One   1

It Takes Two   17

Three Is as Magic as Can Be   35

Four Men on Horses   55

May Day Number Five   79

These Six Walls   85

Seven Colors   97

A Perfect Eight   117

Revolution Nine   135

About the Author

Foreword

What is it about numbers, anyway?

On one hand, we owe them a great deal. Most of humankind's biggest accomplishments can be attributed to numbers. Without their help, we would probably still be trying to build pyramids in Egypt and great walls in China. Seafaring explorers might still be looking for the New World without numbers to guide their navigation; a trip to the moon might remain the stuff of science fiction.

Of course, you don't have to be on the cutting edge of science to see the impact of numbers. To some extent, numbers are an innate part of our wiring as a species. We've been using numbers to measure and communicate for as long as we've been speaking to each other. Today they impact most every aspect of our lives. Your typical day may include waking up in time to head to work, shopping, paying bills, phoning friends and a bevy of other routine activities. Easy, right? Now try doing them without numbers. Not so easy, right?

Numbers bring order. Measure. Perspective.

And yet...

For all the accomplishment and convenience they bring to our lives, many of us fall short of what should be a genuine love affair. At best, we're willing to maintain a friendship only. Often it's uglier than that. Some of us are actually turned off by numbers. If they come at us in the form of statistics, we deeply mistrust them. If they show up in the form of algebra or long division, we avoid them like visits to the dentist, yielding only when we have to. We dreaded Friday the 13th long before Jason Voorhees arrived. For some, numerology helps explain mystical properties associated with numbers. And if it all gets to be too much we may develop arithmophobia, a medically-diagnosed fear of numbers.

Somewhere between the extremes of love and loathing lie the rest of us. A healthy respect for all that numbers do, flavored with a pinch of apprehension for the unknown that they bring.

Numbers bring mystery. Superstition. Fear.

It is also between these two extremes that this collection of short stories sits. Arithmophobia presents nine stories, each based on one of the single digit numbers 1-9. As the building blocks of our number system, most of us have been using these since childhood to assign value, to count, to enumerate. But these numbers have also made their way to the lexicon of society, as well as the literature.

In Arithmophobia, author Ruschelle Dillon subtly examines what's behind curtain numbers 1-9. An author whose style has historically blended horror and humor, Ruschelle calls upon both to ask the question I led this Forward with:

What is it about numbers, anyway?

What is it about the number 1? How can the same number set you apart as the one, and separate you from the rest at the same time? If "1" truly means "only one", what can that combination of responsibility and isolation do? The story "The One" examines these questions.

Ruschelle explores similar questions throughout this collection. For example:

• Can the same number mean both perfection and imperfection? If so, what can such a dichotomy do? The story "Three is a Magic Number" examines this.
• A calendar based on numeric dates simplifies many things; it certainly makes it easy to mark holidays and anniversaries. Can a date held in high regard be used to create something to dread? The story "May Day Number 5" asks this.

•   Why do some numbers appear repeatedly and spontaneously in nature? Is there such a thing as "random design", or does Mother Nature know something we do not? Ask yourself this question as you read both "These Six Walls" and "Seven Colors."

Whether you consider yourself someone who loves, tolerates, or loathes numbers, I think you will find Arithmophobia to be a fascinating and exciting opportunity to wonder about them. Some of the following stories will make you smile, some will make you shudder. But each one will likely leave you wondering "What if?" If nothing else, I suspect this collection will have you joining me in the asking:
What is it about numbers, anyway?

John A. Monaco

Freelance writer and friend (only) of numbers

The One

The words 'one' and 'only' often appear together. But what happens when being the one—the one chosen for something, the one in charge, the one to hold it all together— leads to being the only one? What happens in the place where responsibility and isolation meet?

Adam abruptly returned to consciousness with a snort and a groan. Just minutes earlier he had escaped the here and now, dozing off in his favorite overstuffed armchair while watching *The Matrix*. But an accidental encounter with the volume button on the remote changed all that. On the plus side, he awoke in time to be greeted by his favorite scene: the intense final battle between Neo and Agent Smith.

Adam's wife Kathy, a slip of a blonde, pried the remote from his hand and turned down the blaring audio. She promptly returned the device, making sure it found a painful target when she plopped it back in his lap.

"You fell asleep watching *The Matrix* again. How many times are you gonna watch that movie?"

Adam just snickered. He loved torturing the love of his life, though he made sure never to cross any lines lest she realize she could have married better. He never quite understood why the former beauty pageant winner and swimsuit model chose to settle down with the likes of him. So he always teased with caution. But when dealing with matters of Neo and *The Matrix*, it was hard to suppress his passion.

Still trying to shake off the dust of his afternoon nap, Adam stood and stretched. He made his way to the kitchen, where Kathy had returned to the stack of dirty dishes.

"Kath, you need to give Neo a chance. If you'd just watch it once you'd understand. He is the One! Know why they called him that? Because he is the only one! Just think of it... out of all 7 billion people in the world, he is the only one that can stand up to the horrors of a world ravaged by war. They tried to fool everyone with their computer-generated reality... but only The One could slip past that. He's one in a million! Check that... he's one in 7 billion! He's the One!"

Kathy glared at her husband and threw a dishtowel at his head.

"Tell The One he can start saving the world by drying the dishes."

Adam regarded their spirited bickering as foreplay. Kathy, three months pregnant, did not. Happily married but childless for six years, their lives were transformed when Kathy discovered her bout with food poisoning was actually morning sickness. For the first few weeks they referred to their unborn as 'The Little Blessing.' Now, one trimester into it, a proper name still eluded them. But Kathy wasn't worried. She figured she'd know what to name the child when the time came.

Adam shut the television off and caressed the small bump that was starting to grow in Kathy's formerly model-like flat belly.

"What did you say, Bless? Okay, I'll tell her... Bless just came up with some great ideas for names."

Crossing her arms across her burgeoning breasts, Kathy raised an eyebrow.

"Bless says the name should be Trinity if she has girly parts and Neo if he has boy parts! Wow, Blessy, those are perfect!" He rubbed his wife's belly like he would a Happy Buddha's and gave it a sloppy kiss. She rolled her eyes and returned to the sink.

"You're an adorable mess," she said.

Adam rolled into the church office around 7:00 am, just like every other day. A cup of convenience store coffee and a glazed donut served as inspiration as he tooled his daily sermon. At the age of 22 he had become the youngest minister in Pennsylvania to ever serve a Christian church. Now 10 years into the job, he still felt privileged to hold the position.

Sundays, of course, were work days. And this Sunday morning started off no differently than any other. By 9:51 A.M. Adam was confident that he had affixed the perfect amount of passion to his sermon. Ten minutes later, he found himself at his pulpit, greeting his small congregation with his contagious smile.

Adam's familiarity with the congregation made it easy for him to spot the newcomer. Hunkered down in the last bench at the back of the church, the shabby-looking elderly man sat adorned in multiple layers of ragged brown and olive clothing. His head was bowed as if in deep prayer. Or possibly deep in sleep, Adam thought. An awkward-fitting fur hunting cap was pulled over his eyes, the ear flaps hiding the rest of his face. Adam made a mental note to approach the visitor after the service, and then moved on to deliver his newly-created masterpiece.

As usual, time seemed to fly at the pulpit. The reverend finished his service with his signature statement:

"Until we meet again my brothers and sisters, go with God."

Adam glanced back to the last bench in the back of the church. The visitor was gone. Perhaps he was new to town and needed a quick prayer. Or maybe he was a vagabond needing a place to take a quick nap. He shrugged it off and carried on. There was still work to be done.

As he did every Sunday, Adam made his way to the front doors of the church to mingle with those who had remained. And as she did every Sunday, Ms. Wheatly was the first to approach him. This time, however, her motive was not to exchange pleasantries. Ms. Wheatly shared the startling news about Seth Livingston, a young member of the church. At only 18 years old, Seth had died the day before. The death was sudden and unexpected, and had the entire church buzzing with rumors and speculation.

Adam took the news hard. In all his years of service he had yet to experience the loss of a youthful member of the congregation. Later that afternoon, the Livingston family contacted him to request a funeral service.

Another first for Adam.

Preparations for the funeral kept Adam busy throughout the evening. The alarm screamed a bit too soon for him to even think of waking up, but he knew the convenience store coffee and his congregation was awaiting him. Kissing Kathy good-bye, Adam launched himself apprehensively from bed and prepared for the emotional day ahead.

He arrived at the usual time, and spent the early part of his morning hidden in his office, reflecting and praying. The Livingston family and friends began arriving at 11:30 to privately say their last farewells. This was painfully difficult for Adam to witness; vibrant, steadfast members of his church reduced to raw, fragile mourners. Adam was still young in 'preacher-years'; delivering a funeral service for a congregant still in his teens was a new duty for him. And he was more anxious about doing this than any other pastoral obligation before.

"Sometimes" he thought, "I wish there really was a Matrix; an alternate reality that you can plug into and escape from bad things like this."

Adam closed the casket and made his way to the back of the church. He opened the heavy lead glass doors to receive the supportive community. Among the crowd was Kathy. She smiled reassuringly at Adam, and then quietly took a seat in the back of the church. She should not have been out, but Adam was selfishly happy that, just as always, she was right there with him. Within minutes, the church filled with supporters. Adam nervously took to the pulpit and began the service with a prayer. He then took a pause to collect his thoughts. His voice was replaced with soft sounds of weeping.

Now fifteen minutes into the service, he felt no more at ease than when he first took to the altar. He looked to the back of the church, desperately needing a shot of support from Kathy. She delivered, with that same subtle smile that always seemed to calm his emotions.

Before Adam's eyes could return to his notes, they strayed to the seat behind his wife. There, they found another familiar figure. The visitor from last Sunday's service had returned.

The man resumed his previous position, head lowered in some meditative gaze; body camouflaged by the same fur hunting cap and grungy outfit. His appearance caused Adam to lose his train of thought, as he stammered and stuttered his way through his notes. He could not help but wonder why the man was here. Did he know the family?

As the celebration of Seth's life concluded, the congregation stood in silence while the casket was carried out. As Adam acknowledged his pregnant wife on the way out of the church, his eyes couldn't help but dart to the pew behind her. The stranger had disappeared again.

Adam picked at the dinner Kathy had prepared. It wasn't that he didn't love her cooking, but after an emotionally draining observance he didn't have much of an appetite. The day had thrown him off of his routine, which typically involved parking his cell phone on the kitchen counter before sitting for a meal. Instead it remained in his pocket, which is why he noticed the call: Harold Weibinger. Something compelled him to interrupt dinner and answer, usually a taboo act in Kathy's eyes. But parishioners rarely called him during evening hours unless it was important.

As Adam listened to the voice on the line, he almost wished he had ignored the call. Mrs. Weibinger sobbed through her news report; her husband Harold had just passed away.

During the months that followed, the morbid routine played out; a string of unexpected deaths that rocked the congregation and stretched the limits of coincidence. The count was now at seventeen. Seventeen lives ended, much to the horror of their loved ones. A funeral was held seemingly every few days. The small church in this quiet Pennsylvania town was shaken to its core.

The sheriff and local authorities even felt compelled to attempt an investigation, but it only amounted to asking a few questions. Seventeen deaths in a matter of months among the same church congregation were indeed alarming, but the facts extinguished any cause for alarm. Each had died of natural causes or verified accidents. Tragic and horrific for sure. But nothing criminal.

By this point, Adam was distraught, sleep deprived, and angry. His congregation was dying. There were no joyous events, no weddings, no births. Only death. And yet, amidst his pain and anguish, was the growing obsession over a stranger. The man who now appeared regularly at each Sunday service, at each funeral service. Technically no longer an outsider, Adam nevertheless considered him so. How else could he view him? His exits remained so quick that every attempt to reach him after a service was met with the same failed outcome.

At every service, the silent outsider was present, interacting with no one. He never spoke, never lifted his head from his chest to give anyone the chance to catch a glimpse of what lurked under his ratty fur hat. His presence made Adam edgy. Moreover, he was beginning to question his own sanity. In an ironic twist, Adam wondered if he had in effect become 'The One'... the only one his congregation could turn to in a tragic time. And he began to realize how lonely his movie hero must have felt. The pressure of being the only one is almost too much to bear.

After a particularly gut wrenching funeral for a five-year-old who died of an asthma attack, Adam limped home, laid his head on Kathy's now bulging belly, and prayed for divine intervention.

"Kath, why is this happening? This isn't normal. None of this is normal."

Kathy said nothing. There were no answers to be had.

Adam continued his one-sided discussion.

"What did our little church do to deserve this? I don't know how much more I can take. I never get to see you anymore. The only person I see on a regular basis is that guy in the fur hat. He creeps me out, Kath. I mean, where did he come from? Why is he at our church? Why does he run off before I can introduce myself? I never see him anywhere else in town. Who is this?"

Discussing the man's curious attendance annoyed Adam. Maybe it was annoyance, or maybe fatigue. In any event, he began looking for ways to make sense of all the madness.

"He shows up out of nowhere and *bam*, our congregation is dying." Adam lifted his head from Kathy's stomach and clutched her hand.

"Do you think he could be... Satan? Do you think he is here to punish us? Do you think this is Armageddon?"

Seeing the fear in her husband's eyes, she kissed him on the cheek.

"No dear. He's just a man. And this is just a very bad time for all of us. Hey... I have an idea."

With that, Kathy reached over to the nightstand and pulled out *The Matrix* DVD.

"Let's watch a movie. Together."

Adam smiled for the first time in months. "You mean it?"

Not about to give her a chance to change her mind, Adam leapt from the bed and quickly loaded the DVD. Just as quickly as he left, he returned to Kathy's waiting arms, and escaped reality for a while. As he watched, he occasionally thought again about Neo, and the maddening responsibility of being The One... the only one who could deal with tragic reality. And he wished there really was an alternate reality that he could just plug himself into to escape from his own maddening responsibility. But not tonight. Tonight, there was no place else he'd rather be. He had Kathy. And he had *The Matrix*.

The following Sunday saw a significant decline in attendance for the scheduled service. The recent glut of funerals had even the staunchest worshippers questioning their faith. With bloodshot eyes from lack of sleep, Adam took the pulpit and almost begrudgingly started the service.

"My brothers and sisters, these last few months have taken a toll on us all. We have lost friends and loved ones and our hearts are heavy. But know that they are with our Father in heaven and He..."

His words trailed off when he saw the cryptic man in the brown and olive green clothing, perched in his usual spot. Adam's eyes bored into the mysterious man.

Who is this evil intruder? he thought, as the blood rose in his cheeks. Hoping to smite the apparent devil sitting in front of him, he snatched his Bible from the podium and went on the attack as only a preacher can.

"There is a demon among us in this church, in our family! He is toying with our lives, reveling in our suffering. We opened ourselves up to him and he has done nothing but rip at our hearts and sneer at our souls!" He clutched the Bible to his chest and pointed to the accused.

"You sir, are no longer welcome here. I cast you out. I cast you from this house of worship in the name of our Lord and Savior Jesus Christ! Be gone, devil! Go back to the fiery hell that you came from!"

The congregation watched in silent horror. Was the preacher accusing a member of the church of being a demon? Who was this attack aimed at? Amidst the chaos, the stranger remained stoic, behaving more as a silent spectator than participant. Adam continued his tirade.

"The book of John says:

You are of your father the devil, and your will is to do your father's desires. He was a murderer from the beginning, and has nothing to do with the truth, because there is no truth in him. When he lies, he speaks out of his own character, for he is a liar and the father of lies.

"I command you in the name of God to take your deceit, pain and death and leave this house!"

With that, Adam lunged into the seated congregation, making his way toward the back location of the stranger. It

8

took three church elders to pull Adam from his intended target. Struggling and spitting curses, he was taken to his office. There, he threw himself onto the floor like a defiant child and wept. Months of tension streamed from his eyes. The buzz from the elders and the congregation was that the barrage of funerals must have finally undone their beloved preacher. Most assured themselves that a good day's rest and the power of prayer would bring him back to the fold. In the church, the congregation offered a hasty prayer for their distraught leader. Back in the office, Adam reclaimed his composure, apologized profusely to the elders who accompanied him to this refuge, and pled his case to drive home unaided. It was only with the promise of spending the rest of the day in bed did the elders acquiesce.

Adam sat in the driveway and prayed before going inside. Kathy's pregnancy had her feeling ill and she did not attend the service, a fact Adam was most grateful for. However, he was now faced with the need to explain his ill-timed outburst to her. With the baby so close to delivery, he didn't need her worrying if his erratic behavior would ostracize them from their church family or, worse yet, put him out of a job at the worst possible time. Adam stared at the front door, sighed, "go with God", and started up the sidewalk.

Before laying a hand on the doorknob, he caught sight of someone slipping around the back of his house. Not sure what to believe anymore, he considered that what he saw could be real... or not. But he was convinced that whatever he just saw was wearing an all-too-familiar combination of brown and olive green.

He hurried around to the rear of the house, where the basement door slammed shut just as he approached.

Adam's thoughts raced: *It can't be... he knows where I live? He's in my house! God help me, what do I do? What about Kath and the baby?*

That thought drove Adam to action. He bolted through the door and made his way up the basement stairs.

"You're not taking my family, you bastard."

He seethed as he grabbed a butcher knife from the drawer. He began investigating each room on the first floor, to no avail. He made his way up to the second floor and peered into the master bedroom. The bed was unoccupied but a large bloody smear painted the sheets. Adam began to panic.

"Where is Kath? Did that demon kidnap her?" He tried to call for her, but his tongue and throat refused to cooperate. With each careful step, his heart pounded faster. Suddenly and without warning, the bathroom door swung open. The will to live and protect his family overtook Adam. Weapon in hand, he lunged at the open doorway.

The knife found a target. The blade pierced Kathy in the temple.

Adam watched in horror as the paramedics carried his wife's lifeless body out of the house and into the ambulance. Once the police arrived, Adam told them all about the intruder. Emotions overtook him, and he fell to the floor while trying to explain what happened to Kathy. Apprehensively, officers took advantage of Adam's position to handcuff him.

"I didn't mean to hurt her. She's my wife. I love her. Oh God, what's going to happen to my baby? I want to see my baby. I want to see my wife. Why? Why did he do this to me?"

A small crowd of neighbors had assembled in front of Adam's house. He could almost hear the gossip emanating from under their collective breath as he sat handcuffed in the back of the police car, his clothes stained with blood. Oddly, he now found himself again thinking about his beloved *Matrix* movie. How he wished there was a false reality he could escape to.

As if on cue, dressed in brown and olive green, the demon appeared; motionless amid the gaggle of gossipmongers. Adam pressed his face hard against the glass and pounded on the cage barrier.

"Hey, he's out there. He's in front of my house. Get him before he gets away. He's right out there! He's got a fur hunting cap on. Go get him!"

The cops rushed from the car and were immediately swallowed up by the chattering horde of bodies.

"He's there. You have to find him," he yelled as he blinked his eyes, trying to stop the tears from blurring the vision of his nemesis who had since been absorbed deep within the bowels of the crowd.

"No no no! Where is he? He was just here. Damn it. He was just here. Where are you? Lord Jesus, help me. Where are you...?"

His prayer was answered. Standing in front of the police cruiser was the demon. Pounding on the windows, Adam shrieked.

"He's here! He's here! Help me, damn it. He's right here!"

His pleas fell on deaf ears. The officers were busy securing the crime scene, too busy to notice Adam's frenzied antics in the back of the cruiser. The demon turned to face his adversary. His head hung low so that only the top of his fur cap was visible.

"What do you want from me?" Adam begged. "Here I am. Are you happy? Is this what you wanted? Is it? My wife is dead because of you. Dead! Do you even care?"

Adam lunged again at the barrier as if he could ram his way through and smash the windshield to tear the demon apart with his cuffed hands.

"Who the hell are you?" he screamed, now too distraught to even realize how un-preacher-like his language had become.

A knock at the rear window seized Adam's attention. After finding no evidence of the man who broke into Adam's house, the officers dispersed the swarm of curiosity seekers and returned to the cruiser. Adam opened his mouth to alert them of the demon's presence. However, as he had always been so prone to do at church, the mysterious man was gone. Defeated, Adam rode in silence as the cruiser made its way to the hospital.

"I want to see my wife. Where is she? I need to see her," Adam roared at the roomful of nurses and doctors trying to wrestle him onto the exam table.

"Calm down, sir. You really need to calm down," begged a Weeble-shaped nurse. A syringe containing what Adam assumed was a sedative was clenched in her hand. Adam grabbed her thick wrist.

"You don't understand... she's carrying our baby. I want to see my baby. Is my baby okay? Please tell me my baby is okay."

"Look, sir, we'll check on your wife and baby as soon as you calm down and let us examine you. So, settle down and let us do our job."

Settling down was close to impossible, but Adam knew if he was going to see his newborn Blessing, he would need to do as the medics prescribed. So he stopped resisting, took his place on the table, and closed his eyes.

"Just tell me when you're finished, because I want to see my baby."

Adam jolted at the sounds of metal clanging and voices shouting nefarious instructions. Frantically, he scanned the room to determine what was happening. He was handcuffed to his bed. He was cold. The room was sterile. His eyes caught the words printed on the door: COUNTY MORGUE.

A team of doctors and nurses had their hands and instruments plunged in the abdominal cavity of his dead wife. The horror of the scene was almost too much for him to process.

"Kathy! I'm sorry. I'm so sorry."

He continued his pleas for mercy as the macabre scene continued to play out in front of him. Those pleas fell on deaf ears, as the team was busy cutting and sucking the dead flesh and putrefying fluids from her body to get to the child. What made the scene grislier was the fact that the team was literally bathed in his wife's blood. In fact, the morgue itself was flooded with what seemed liked gallons of blood. Adam threw himself back onto his pillow and bawled. The lead doctor's voice boomed through the stark morgue.

"Ahhh... there we are. We got him out just in time."

Him! Did I hear the doctor say 'him'? Adam thought as his bed was wheeled closer to the horrific display.

"I want to see him. I want to see my boy." One of the nurses had taken the child over to the sink to clean him up.

"Please let me hold my boy."

The doctor pulled down his bloody mask and smiled.

"He's a good one. Strong too. He'll be perfect for our needs."

Adam propped himself up on his elbows again.

"What are you talking about? Your needs? What needs?"

"Here he is" the doctor continued. "Say hello and goodbye to your son, Reverend. Nurse, please be sure to jack that little one in."

The nurse held up Adam's son so he could see him. Adam again opened his mouth to scream, but nothing came out. From the back of his infant son's neck was a hole in which the doctor jammed a large metal socket. Grinning like the Cheshire cat, the doctor sneered.

"He's gonna love *The Matrix*, isn't he, Reverend? Oh, don't worry... we've written up a great life for him. He's going to be a computer programmer... for a large computing firm. He may not be The One, the... how do you like to put it... 'one in seven billion'? Well, he won't be anything like that. But he won't be alone either, like you. He's going to be very satisfied."

Adam awoke handcuffed to a gurney in a drab hospital room. Two of the elders were waiting for him to waken from the sedative so that they could discuss the day's grim events with him. Adam rallied.

"Where's my son? They took my son! Where is he?"

The elders eyeballed each other. There was no way Adam could have known he had a son. The sedative had just worn off and the baby had been taken hours ago.

One of the elders—Elder Thomas—took Adam by the hand.

"Adam, I'm so sorry, but... your son, well... he didn't make it. The doctors thought they got to him in time... and... he did hang in there for a little while, but... he just wasn't strong enough. He's gone to be with Kathy. He's gone to be with Our Heavenly Father."

"God help me" Adam thought. "I've lost everything... including my mind."

Over the course of the next two days, Adam's church family took turns staying with him in the hospital. They discussed his upcoming hearing and prayed together that there would be no prison sentence. Most surmised that he was under a great deal of stress and—at least in their biased view—he had clearly acted in self-defense.

Under judicious sedation, doctors and officials agreed that Adam should be permitted to attend the joint funeral of his wife and his newborn son. Walking into the church, Adam noticed the congregation had dwindled even more since he left of his post. The sparse church members in attendance appeared overwhelmed, downtrodden and dazed. The church itself seemed worn and battered, as if it had been abandoned or caught in the crossfire of battle. He lamented that had failed his church too.

None of that seemed to matter now. All that mattered was Kathy. Now all he wanted was to see that subtle smile one more time. All he wanted was to tell her that he loved her; that there was no other woman like her. With the help of Elder Thomas, Adam inched his way toward the caskets. The tears burned his eyes. Paying their respects to the deceased, the small gathering parted for Adam and let him through to the matching pearl and gold decked caskets in the front of the church. He stopped three feet from the bodies, grabbed his head and howled.

"You son of a bitch... *get out of there*! Get off of my wife!"

Adam leapt into the casket and grabbed the body of the demon—still bound from head to toe in brown and olive green wraps—and shook him violently.

"Who the hell are you? What do you want from me?" A small mob of men grabbed Adam by the shoulders and attempted to rend the lifeless body from his hands.

"Don't you see what this demon has done? He's taken everyone we love away from us. He's the one who is killing our families. He's the one who killed my Kathy."

Wrestling the corpse away from Adam, the casket overturned. Kathy's remains fell to the floor. The church rang with horrified screams. Adam punched and pounded the corpse, eventually knocking over the tiny casket holding his son. He lurched for his child, but was restrained by Thomas and a police officer.

"Let me see my son! Check his neck... check his neck!" The men subdued Adam and drug him screeching down the isle of the church.

"They've plugged him into the Matrix! Check his neck. Check it. Check it. Check it!"

The old man returned to consciousness with a snort and a groan. Just minutes earlier, he had escaped the here and now, dozing off while reading "The Matrix." He preferred the movie version—a theatrical obsession of his, actually—but electronic devices like televisions and DVD players had been long since rendered useless.

As he attempted to shake off the dust of an afternoon nap, he scanned his surroundings. As he often did this time of day, he had made his way into a church. A lonely pew nestled in the back row was where he had taken his latest rest. Churches were among the few buildings still standing, and they offered adequate shelter from the nuclear winter conditions outdoors.

Not that it was much warmer inside. He buttoned his ragged brown and olive green jacket and pulled his fur hunting cap over his ears before continuing his visual tour of the place.

He squinted to read a sign that barely clung to the pulpit at the front of the church. It read "Until we meet again my brothers and sisters, go with God." —REV. ADAM.

Why thank you, Reverend Adam, he thought to himself. *We Adams need to stick together.*

From his coat pocket he pulled out one of his most prized possessions; a tattered few pages from a fashion magazine. On them, a photo shoot of a swimsuit model. Among the images were shots of the blonde beauty donned in pageant paraphernalia. The old man had taken to calling her "Kathy." In a desolate world such as this, a few pages from a magazine were sufficient to fall in love.

"Nice place, huh Kath?"

He continued staring at his surroundings. The old church had probably seen better days. Like many other buildings that remained, it looked battered... abandoned after being caught in the crossfire of battle.

He moved a lot each day, looking for others and sleeping where he could. The war had left the world in shambles, so this church and others like it were a welcome respite from the harsh realities of desolation. He liked imagining the pews full of people. Not that he would know what to do if he saw any. It had been many years now. He'd seen so many die in those first few months. Now everyone else was apparently gone. He was alone, most likely the only one left. All he had was his Matrix book. And Kathy.

Of course, he also had the dreams. They seemed to grow more odd, and yet somehow more realistic, each time. If he didn't know better, he'd believe he really was plugging into another reality with each one. In today's dream, he was the respected leader of a church much like this one. He had Kathy by his side, carrying his baby. But someone didn't want him there. He couldn't remember all the details, but he knew there was something wrong. He was not supposed to be there. That happened a lot in his dreams.

On the other hand, he considered that maybe he had simply gone mad. Years of loneliness and isolation may indeed have torn away his sanity, leaving him "an adorable mess," as his mother used to call him.

There is a place where being The One—the only one of seven billion—makes you a hero. But in this place, being the only one makes you something else. Old Adam wasn't sure exactly what.

"But Kath," he said, carefully folding the old magazine photos and returning them to his pocket, "I suppose we've got plenty of time to figure it all out."

It Takes Two

Vanity can lead us down some scary paths. And while medical science continues to change the rules of physical beauty, what if our vanity were to leave us vulnerable to one of the universal rules of biology; the one suggesting that it takes two?

Ahnna glared into the floor length mirror at her newly-Botoxed face and tried to grimace. Her manicured hands ignored the freshly plumped cheeks and lips that her husband Carmen, the "Donut-King", had recently funded. Instead, she swigged some Cristal, clamped a silk-wrapped claw onto her breast, and seethed, "These tiny bitches have got to go."

Only 25 years old, Ahnna was already widowed and remarried. Her current husband was a man she deemed physically repulsive but monetarily sexy: a man thirty years her senior who owned and operated a chain of upscale donut shops across the Mid-Atlantic States. With money comes great responsibility. Keeping up with the Kardashians and looking beautiful was a full-time job, and Ahnna was the consummate workhorse.

The plastic surgeon's office was small but tastefully decorated. Hues of soft grey and eggshell covered the walls, while modern metal art pieces and minimalist furniture conveyed a trendy gallery feel. Ahnna eagerly awaited her appointment amid a collection of plasticized women in various degrees of 'assembly.' As she waited, she sized up most of the results around her. She could not help but be impressed with the skilled hands of the city's hottest new surgeon. The nurse, whose nametag read "Evita", was a perfect walking billboard for the doctor's talents. She invited Ahnna into a cozy examination room, where she took Ahnna's vitals and read over her medical history. Evita then led Ahnna to the doctor's personal office to discuss options. As she did, she caught Ahnna's eyes fixating on her own artfully sculpted masterpieces and gave her a wink.

"Doctor Ivan does beautiful work, don't you think?"

The nurse turned toward Ahnna and pushed her breasts forward, as if offering an appetizer tray to a party guest.

"My breasts were a size A cup before my procedure. And now? Now they are a size C, and still growing!"

"Still... growing?"

"Yes, still growing. I'll let the doctor explain the details, but what makes his work so unique is an advanced breast augmentation technique that he has developed. The procedure is quicker than traditional surgery and near painless. And the best part of all is that your breasts grow naturally. No one needs be the topic of social circles or 'did she or didn't she?' type gossip. The augmentation happens gradually, with two small biological organic implants. So it's not as much shock to the body either. Your body gradually learns to accept what is implanted, so there is much less chance of rejection."

Ahnna protectively reached for her own AA's. "Well, how will they know to stop growing?"

The nurse smiled, "I'm not the doctor, but I assure you, they just do. This procedure is revolutionary and is intended for women who desire full, voluptuous breasts." In a comforting gesture, the nurse leaned forward and placed her hand on Ahnna's knee. "Between us girls... if you want the most beautiful bosom a woman can have without all the painful bruising, lengthy recovery time, and infuriating gossip, then this procedure is *definitely* for you."

Ahnna glowered at the sight of Evita's hand on her overpriced designer jeans. Sensing her faux pas, the nurse pulled her hand from Ahnna's ensemble and hastily handed her a brochure touting the benefits of the cutting-edge technology. At the same time, Dr. Ivan breezed into his office, snatched Ahnna's medical file from his buxom creation, and plopped himself behind his twisted metal and Plexiglas desk. Evita seized her moment and left the doctor to his indignant patient.

The doctor leaned across his desktop to get a better look at Ahnna's assets. It made Ahnna uncomfortable. She didn't relish her small breasts being ogled by men, even if they were professionals in the art of enhancement. She crossed her arms across her chest.

"Explain to me your new technique. Your nurse said they... grow?"

The doctor leapt from his sadistic looking chair and landed in front of Ahnna. His freakish smile and oversized teeth made her cringe.

He rubbed his bony hands together and proclaimed, "Ahnna, the procedure is advanced; it's sound. I've spent years perfecting it. Surgeons around the world want insight into my approach."

He bowed closer to Ahnna and purred, "Actually, it's quite simple."

Ahnna shifted stiffly in her seat. Her buttocks were starting to fall asleep from sitting so long. Noticing her discomfort, he invited her to stand. As she warily stood in front of him, his huge paws forced her shoulders back, correcting her posture. Before she could protest, he swiftly slid two fingers over her cashmere sweater and rested them under the cups of her push-up bra.

"Now, under each breast, we form a tiny incision no bigger than a bug bite. It is here that we insert a small organic 'seed.' This seed will work with your body. You will be required to eat a special diet of foods and supplements, which we supply. These will gradually blossom into a full, luxurious pair of breasts. The pair that nature failed to grant you."

Ahnna stepped back to create some distance between 'the girls' and the doctor's prying hands; her maneuver led her to fall back into her chair. She understood the hands-on nature of plastic surgeons, but that didn't mean she enjoyed it. Unfazed by Ahnna's behavior, Dr. Ivan continued his campaign. He seemed to know just what angle to take with Ahnna.

"Ahnna, based on your medical records you are a prime candidate for this procedure. Of course, many people avoid it because, well, it is rather expensive and..."

Ahnna cut him off, offended at the notion that cost would matter to her. "Money won't be an issue. I'll expect results, though. I want to look like Nurse Elvira out there."

"Evita? Yes, she's a dear. And we're both quite proud of her results. But I'm rather certain that I can give you a pair that will rival hers. I will personally select the two that will join you."

"The two that will join me?"

"Forgive my choice of words," Dr. Ivan explained, "I take my work so personally that I sometimes get a little dramatic about it. The two organic seeds that will be inserted. I will select them personally to make sure you get off to the best start possible."

Ahnna was used to finding others to be odd. It came with thinking she was better than others, even if she'd have to pay extra to get there.

"That's fine. I'll pay your price."

"Very good then" said the doctor, trying to subdue the enthusiasm that came from sealing a deal. "But I have one important question to ask you before we can proceed, and you need to be completely honest when answering."

Ahnna looked puzzled. She'd learned over the years that a setup like that usually meant the need to lie.

"Do you drink alcohol?"

"Shit," Ahnna thought. She loved her wine... and her bourbon... and her vodka. But what could it hurt? Maybe she could stave off the booze for a little while. So she lied.

"No."

"Fantastic!" He gleefully noted her records. "I would love to set you up with a beautiful new you. Unfortunately, I'm booked solid for six months, but you don't seem like a woman who waits for anything."

Ahnna's heart sank. Preparing to make a defiant exit, she gripped the arms of her chair.

"Six months is too long to wait. I can always find someone else."

Knowing this would be her response, Dr. Ivan repeated his previous point.

"As I stated, you don't seem like a woman who waits for anything. I had a cancellation for 4:00 this afternoon. I realize that's short notice, but the time slot is yours if you want it. If you need to speak with your husband first, I understand. But this opportunity won't last for very long."

Ahnna snorted. "Ah yes, my husband..."

For the third time this month, the Donut King was in Las Vegas for a "marketing convention." He wouldn't be back until the end of the week. He had *his* addictions and so did Ahnna.

"My husband doesn't make decisions about my body." Ahnna glanced at her platinum and diamond Movado watch. It was ten of two.

"Four o'clock? Fine. Where do I sign?"

The doctor bared his bizarrely large teeth at Ahnna. "You've made a fantastic decision. One that every woman in that waiting room wishes they could make. My nurse will be in to discuss post-care foods and supplements with you. By then, we'll be ready to prep you for surgery."

Ahnna's eyes popped open in the recovery room at 4:35. She attempted to feel her new breasts, but met resistance from nurse Evita.

"Ah ah. No touching for at least a day, dear. Give them time to heal without fussing with them. You'll be up and out of here in a few minutes. I'll get everything ready for your release." She opened the door to leave, but stopped short. "Ahnna, you're going to be so happy with them." Ahnna eyes rolled back into her head; the sound of sales-pitch chatter lulled her back into unconsciousness.

It was barely a week after surgery, and the only hint of change in Ahnna was a dull ache under each breast where the "seeds" had been implanted. The nurse was right. There was no extraordinary pain, no swelling and no bruising. If she didn't see the tiny incisions under her breasts, she would have questioned whether or not she had even gone under the knife. Each morning she stood naked in front of her bedroom mirror, hoping to catch any sign of blossoming. But so far, nothing. Her post-surgery regimen of two capsules twice a day, plus a disconcerting diet of nothing but sludgy protein shakes, was wearing thin. Worse, post-care dictated detoxing from all alcohol, and Ahnna desperately wanted a glass—or better yet a bottle—of Pinot. Ahnna's patience was waning, and she began to second guess her decision. Was this a con job? Had she been taken advantage of because of her wealth and vanity?

Ahnna snatched her cell phone. And after a few rings, Nurse Evita answered in an upbeat and bubbly tone. But Ahnna was eager for a brawl. She skipped the pleasantries and cut right to the chase.

"This is Ahnna. It's not working. They're not growing. It's been almost a week, and nothing! Do you know who you're fucking with? If this is some kind of sick joke, I will sue you. All of you!"

Ahnna could hear the grating smile in the nurse's reply.

"Ahnna, I assure you this is not some 'sick joke.' This is a fantastic marriage of biology and technology. You chose this procedure because it was a more natural method of breast enhancement. I can understand being a bit anxious..."

"Can you?" Ahnna spewed.

"Yes, Ahnna. I understand exactly how you feel. I promise you, in two full months you will have the breasts you've always wanted. Mine are still growing and should be at their peak in just a few more weeks. Maybe the doctor will let you start the next phase of the diet plan a little early. That's when you'll start seeing them bloom. I tell you what... if you hold, I'll ask him."

Ahnna was in no mood to wait.

"No, I'm through waiting. Just tell me. I'm sick of drinking nothing but these horrible shakes. I want a damn glass of wine. Take me to the next phase now!"

Evita hesitated.

"Well, I should really speak with..."

"Damn it! A few days won't make a frigging bit of difference. What do I have to do?"

"Okay, Ahnna. Grab a pen and paper. I have a list of foods for you."

Ahnna was thrilled to be eating solid food again. She gobbled down the protein-heavy fare the diet recommended and looked forward to each meal. Except for lunch. Lunch still consisted of those shakes and supplements she had grown to hate. But now, fourteen days after surgery, there was finally a breakthrough.

Ahnna's breasts had prospered to a respectable B cup. With a change in appearance came a change in attitude. Ahnna even found herself anticipating her husband's homecoming to show off her swelling new features.

"Hell, I might even let him play with them... if I knock back a drink or two first," she thought to herself.

And there lay the rub. Of all the things she could do to celebrate the first signs of post-procedure success, the one that seemed the most appealing to her was a toast. But alcohol was still off limits. The stocked bar relentlessly taunted her.

"This is bullshit," Ahnna complained to herself. "One drink. That's all I need, is one drink. It's been days, dammit. I can handle one drink."

In reality, fourteen days was the longest Ahnna had gone since high school without as much as a taste of bourbon ripping through her veins. One drink would satisfy her dependence. One drink would keep her sane.

Ahnna stared down a bottle of unopened Shiraz, but instead poured a conservative shot of her favorite rye bourbon. She rationalized it would be a waste to open a new bottle for a sole glass of wine. And wasting wine was a sin in her book. She proudly toasted herself in the mirror.

"This one's for you, girls. Make mama proud."

She parted her slightly deflated fish lips and fired the shot down her throat. She gazed back into the mirror and hugged the empty shot glass to her burgeoning breasts.

"I really missed you, Jim. What's that, girls? What are you saying? Oh no. No, I couldn't. I said only one drink." Ahnna mockingly cocked an ear towards her chest.

"But, there are two of you?" I know, I know, but I wasn't supposed to have *one* drink, let alone two. Well, I don't want to play favorites. I love you both equally." Ahnna tipped a second shot, sucked it down her gullet, and nonchalantly poured another.

Ahnna awoke face down on the kitchen floor, accompanied by an empty bottle of bourbon. Her head and breasts ached as she crawled to the refrigerator for something cold and wet. She pulled herself up to the middle shelf, grabbed a bottle of iced tea and held it to her throbbing bosom. She winced and hurled it to the marble floor. Behind the tea sat a package of raw rib eyes in an oniony sweet marinade. Ahnna poked the bag and scowled.

"Jesus," she mumbled. "Why the hell does this look so... delicious?"

Snatching it from the shelf, Ahnna ripped back the cling wrap and gorged herself on the uncooked meat, sticky marinade dripping down her chin as her perfect veneers tore into the softened fibers. With the hunger and ferocity of a starving lion, she devoured all four steaks while hunched in front of the open fridge. When she had finished feasting, she wiped her marinade and blood-stained hands on her Juicy Couture sweat pants and dove back into the fridge, on a hunt for other pre-packaged prey.

Ahnna scored a small package of ground burger almost a month past its expiration date. She cradled the butcher paper in her hands like a newborn kitten, and buried her nose deep into the aroma of decaying meat. It smelled sweet and intoxicating. Ahnna clawed through the paper and dug into the fetid burger. The barely-chewed beef slid effortlessly down her throat. She consumed only a few handfuls of 85/15 when she felt a sweaty hand grab her arm and yank her up off the floor, almost dislocating her shoulder.

"Ahnna! What the fuck are you eating? What the hell is wrong with you?" Her absentee husband Carmen wrenched a bloody helping from her fingers. "This is raw fucking meat. Raw meat! Look at me, Ahnna." Then, he spied the drained liquor bottle.

"Are you drunk?" Even as he spoke, his eyes turned their attention to her upgraded goods. He grabbed her left marinade-stained breast.

"So you had your fucking boobs done, and you're high on painkillers and alcohol? Is that right? Well, is it?" Ahnna glowered at his unwelcome hand. "Ahnna, you are so fucked up that you are eating raw meat."

Ahnna stared at her husband. She could feel the anger bubbling from the pit of her stomach. She balled a sticky fist, gearing up to punch him in his face. The bastard took her quarry and mauled her tit, and she would have none of it. But instead of hitting him, the reality of the situation hit her. Raw meat?

What came bubbling up wasn't anger, but warm red chunks of undigested bovine. And it made its debut over herself, all over the kitchen floor, and all over the Donut King.

"What the fuck is happening to me?" she whimpered as she steadied herself on the granite island countertop.

"Jesus Christ, Ahnna! Look what the hell you've done."

Ahnna didn't hear him. Instead, she stared at all the gore spewed on the countertop. Although nauseated by the thought of consuming raw meat, she couldn't shake the thought that she had relished each and every bite. It tasted wonderful to her. In a daze, she ran a chipped fingernail through the bile and carnage.

Grabbing her by the shoulders, her husband roared "What is wrong with you, Ahnna?"

Ahnna stared at a lump of regurgitated flesh hanging from her husband's crooked nose. She couldn't believe it herself, but the sight of it made her feel...hungry. She leaned in as if to kiss him but instead licked the bit of meat from his nose and continued licking remains from his face. He shoved her hard into the stove.

"Christ, Ahnna! Stop it."

Ahnna ignored him. Like a fast moving zombie from the movies, she lunged to the countertop and began lapping up the mess. Fighting the urge to vomit himself, the Donut King grabbed her from behind and attempted to prevent her from slurping up any more of her own sickening waste.

"No! I'm not finished!" Ahnna whined like a spoiled child as she tried to tear into his arms with her once impressive nails.

"Stop fighting me, Ahnna. You're sick. You're getting a shower and going to bed. You need to sleep this shit off."

Once tossed in the shower, Ahnna stopped fighting. She let the water overtake her while Carmen also stood naked in the shower scrubbing the vile stink from his skin. He made sure to dutifully bathe her magnificent new breasts, carefully inspecting his latest investment. As he toweled her off, he noticed the wee incisions and was impressed with the skilled surgeons' hand that could implant full C cups into incisions so diminutive. Tucking her naked body into their California King, he bent to kiss her on the forehead, but the image of her earlier behavior killed the moment. Ahnna stirred as he turned off the light.

"Hey. Do you like 'em?"

He stopped at the bedroom door and smirked. "Yeah. They're nice," he replied. "But you should have went bigger."

Ahnna roused gripping her breasts. They felt heavy and sore. "Did someone use my tits as speed bumps last night?" she thought. In reality, what she was feeling was a bad case of growing pains. Her breasts had grown a full cup size in 24 hours.

"Do you drink alcohol?" Now Ahnna understood the earlier question from Dr. Ivan. Apparently alcohol was some sort of catalyst. On the one hand, she was thrilled with the rapid consequence. On the other, she was also worried. This growth couldn't be normal, could it?

Moreover, Ahnna's ordeal from last night disturbed her. At least what she could remember of it. Reluctantly 'drying out' for beautiful breasts only increased her enthusiasm for a binge. But she wondered how she could get so bad that she would behave like that. And while she loved a good steak, the sudden craving was more than that. It was visceral. She didn't just want *meat*; she craved rare, bloody flesh. And it frightened her.

Ahnna stuffed herself into a shirt three sizes too small for her bulging breasts and threw a coat over it to shield anyone from her ill-fitting designer ensemble. She knew she needed to visit Dr. Ivan.

Her thoughts raced as she made her way to the doctor's office. How could they not tell her about the cravings? It was irresponsible and unethical. Sure, she had a drink or ten—under specific direction NOT to drink alcohol—but blood lust was never once mentioned as a side-effect.

Ahnna jetted into the doctor's office as quickly as her hangover would allow. A painfully sylphlike nurse with almost non-existent breasts trailed her as she bypassed the waiting area and buzzed through the doors to the doctor's private office. Dr. Ivan wasn't sitting behind his sterile desk, which angered Ahnna even more. Undeterred, Ahnna spun around and confronted the unfamiliar nurse.

"Where's the doctor?" She glanced at the nurse's unremarkable bosom. "And where is... what's her name? The nurse with the big tits? I need to speak to her right away."

The new nurse grinned. "Oh, you must mean Evita. She's left us. I'm her replacement. How can I help you? My name is Terri."

Ahnna cut her off. "I don't give two shits what your name is. What I do care about is why my boob job is making me want to eat raw meat. No one told me anything about that bullshit."

The nurse looked concerned and attempted to talk Ahnna down. "Ma'am..."

Ahnna's tongue struck her. "It's Ahnna DeVole."

Terri launched into the doctor's personal file cabinets. "I'm sorry. Ahnna. Did you drink any alcohol? Alcohol is not allowed while the implants are maturing. That might be the root of your cravings."

Ahnna bit her puffy lip and snarled "I wouldn't have touched any alcohol if someone had told me the consequences. That's just unprofessional and unacceptable."

The nurse found Ahnna's file and quickly scanned its contents. "It says here that on the day of your consultation, you stated that you didn't drink. You wouldn't have been a candidate for this particular procedure if you'd mentioned that you drink."

Ahnna's lie had come back to haunt her. She'd learned over the years that when caught lying, there's only one thing to do; repeat as necessary.

"Well, it was only one drink. But I should have been properly advised. So how long will these disgusting cravings last?"

The nurse sighed. "Well, they'll last until the maturing period is complete. And by the looks of your progress, it shouldn't be too much longer. So just be patient. The alcohol accelerated the seeds' growth, but in doing so it also interacted with the supplements and caused your regrettable side effect. It may be disconcerting, but you'll be fine.

"You have nothing to worry about, Ahnna. The doctor is just out of this world. You should consider yourself lucky to be chosen for such a beautiful, well... opportunity. Oh and the doctor isn't in today. So I hope I've answered all your questions."

Ahnna bristled as she stomped out the door. "I guess it'll have to do."

Ahnna's Lexus strayed toward the shopping district, where she picked up a few new shirts and blouses to better accentuate her newborn curves. Before long, the shopping therapy was working magic not only on her psyche, but on her hangover as well. She found herself feeling better and feeling hungry. She shimmied into an Italian linen tank top and decided to enjoy the rest of her afternoon dining on sushi at an outside bistro. It wasn't bloody, she thought, but it was raw and socially acceptable. A party of silicone-enhanced "frenemies" spotted Ahnna harvesting a sliver of sashimi from her cleavage. Like a pack of Chihuahuas stalking an unsuspecting hot dog, they all snapped and attacked.

"Ahnna. You look fantastic."

"Where'd you get those done?"

"They look so natural."

"Why didn't you tell us?"

Ahnna swallowed the fatty tuna and painted on an unnatural smile. She wasn't ready to hang with her friends yet, especially after last night's debacle. Unfortunately for Ahnna, her table for one quickly became a table for five. Once a round of drinks was ordered, there was no escape.

While her uninvited guests were downing dirty martinis, Ahnna was actually content sipping mineral water with a twist of lime. That is, until someone ordered a bottle of 1998 Dom Perignon Rose.

"Christ, not the good stuff," Ahnna whispered to herself. "Okay, just one glass... ah, bullshit." Ahnna knew she wasn't going to stop at one glass. It was Dom Perignon.

The bottle was immediately drained, and less costly bottles of champagne were ordered as replacements. Ahnna's urge for meat grew as she tossed back drink after drink. The sushi just wasn't cutting it. And to add insult to injury, the table in front of her was seducing her blood-lust with prime rib. She watched as the customer sliced piece after piece of flesh, knowing that it was softening between his teeth. She could almost feel him relishing the pulp and juices slipping down his throat, satiating his hunger. In a desperate response, Ahnna grabbed a bottle of champagne and began to chug it. Her table just watched in horror. Ahnna slammed the empty bottle down and leered at her latest nemesis' half-eaten plate. The behavior didn't go unnoticed by her compatriots, who by now were feeling their own effects from all the alcohol. One of them decided to call Ahnna out.

"Bitch, what is your problem?"

The grievance wasn't heard. Ahnna lunged at the man's plate and snatched the remaining prime rib, plucking off the globs of fat with her incisors and gobbling up the sweet tissue. The man watched incredulously as his dinner disappeared in the clutches of his new tablemate. His eyes trailed to the beef juices that had stained her tank top. It wasn't the size of her two dirtied breasts that freaked him out. It was the way they moved. It was the *fact* that they moved.

One of her clique had also noticed the undulating from within Ahnna's breasts and, in her drunken stupor, grabbed a fistful of them. As she realized they were really moving, she let out a scream. There was something twisting and lurching underneath Ahnna's skin. Everyone stood in horror and disbelief as Ahnna's breasts freakishly rolled toward one another, almost as if trying to merge with the opposing gland. Ahnna knocked over most of the empty glasses and bottles in her struggle to escape the small crowd that had assembled.

The drive home was an anxious and dangerous one for Ahnna. The combination of alcohol and animated breasts made it nearly impossible to concentrate on the road. And all Ahnna could think about was getting home, away from prying eyes and gossip. Once there, Ahnna violently flung the door open and headed straight to the bar. This was a nightmare, and Ahnna needed to cope the only way she knew how; by crawling further into the bottle.

With drink in hand, she staggered out to the kitchen and found her husband brewing a pot of tea. His mouth dropped when he saw Ahnna's breasts, which had tripled in size since the night before and were dancing and pounding as if to an inaudible drum. The Donut King seized Ahnna by the shoulders and screamed in her face.

"What the hell is going on? Jesus, Ahnna, we're going to the hospital right now."

"No! I'm not going anywhere like this. Leave me alone!"

She jerked herself from his white-knuckled grip, accidently slamming into the corner of the island. That's when she heard it rip. The underside of her monstrous left breast suddenly felt warm and gooey.

"What the hell is happening to me?" Ahnna shrieked as she stared at the blood trickling from her fingers.

Petrified, her husband could only watch as his wife's breast stretched and pulsated from the inside out. A few times, he thought he could make out a little fist punching through Ahnna's skin. He couldn't believe the eerie images assaulting his eyes. Ahnna had sunk to her knees and was drooling through an intense surge of pain.

"What is this? What's happening?" she shrieked. A huge tear was threatening to split apart her right nipple. Carmen grabbed a kitchen towel and clenched Ahnna's deteriorating gland, hoping to secure the breach. Just then a white heat seared through his hand. Screaming garbled expletives, he glimpsed at his palm. His thumb had been ripped from his hand, leaving a horrible gaping wound. He wrapped the already blood-soaked towel around his hand and fought the urge to scream. Though his eyes were tearing from the pain, he caught sight of something jutting from Ahnna's ruptured nipple. He leaned over to inspect the scene of the crime, and was horrified to see a set of spiny black teeth chewing its way out of Ahnna's flesh.

The tea kettle joined the riotous shrieks filling the room. The blood vessels in Ahnna's eye had burst, and blood gushed from her nose and mouth. Her body, no longer under her control, was thrashing and twisting. Her designer slacks, ruined from her bowels and bladder exploding, were now leaking onto the kitchen floor. The Donut King dug his heels in his wife's filth and pushed himself from her quaking body, backing himself into the stove. Within seconds Ahnna's breasts burst open, slinging pieces of bloody tissue throughout the kitchen.

From the carnage, two black skeletal creatures emerged, one from each shattered mammary. Finally able to reach each other, they wasted little time. At their first sight of each other their teeth clicked, and their slender fingers reached out to stroke their new mate.

The King found his voice at the sight of the creatures that erupted from his wife's ruined body. His screams garnered their attention. They snapped their teeth together in a chilling conversation, and attacked.

Convincing his legs to stand, Carmen snatched the tea kettle from the stove and unleashed the boiling water on the horrid little monsters. Their spindly legs buckled under them, slowing them down, but only for a second. The King swung at the beasts with the empty kettle as they shredded his body. The newborn creatures swiftly took down their prey, stripping his body to bone and lapping up very drop of spattered blood.

The back door to Ahnna and the Donut King's house opened at 2:30 A.M. Nurse Terri, who had last seen Ahnna, stepped inside. She found the devastated body and squealed. The children were nestled in the chest cavity of their surrogate mom and were copulating.

"Look, my love. They're so beautiful."

Doctor Ivan stepped in and stroked her cheek with his long bony finger. "The collateral damage will be a revered part of a new history." He looked upon the sight inside and nearly squealed himself before continuing.

"And these two, they will be the authors of that history. It is beyond comprehension to consider that their kind was nearly eliminated. A beautiful race, nearly obliterated by the ignorance of those who would call themselves superior. And all in the name of sport. But here... in this place, on this planet, history begins anew for them. Life begins anew. And all life needs to create more life is..."

Dr. Ivan paused to compose himself, as emotions nearly got the better of him. He looked lovingly at the two creatures and continued.

"All life needs to create more life is two. It takes two to make another. It is true throughout the universe. We have seen it in every corner of the galaxy that we've visited, with every species we have worked to save. Where two join, life can continue. Two can make one. And as long as that is true, the circle of life can carry on."

The doctor peered into Ahnna's mauled body, proudly watching the children continue to mate.

"These humans and their vanity... it made this one almost too easy. Particularly with this woman. Bringing the group here was a wise choice. A planet filled with two-breasted females, eager to make themselves better. Instead, they will make this ancient race better. Their vanity will save others. They will allow us a large supply of working hosts, each with two cocoons, so that our little ones can remain within the very same host, a requirement to make them natural mates when their time comes."

Dr. Ivan took one more look around at the gruesome surroundings. "We will, however, need to do something about this alcohol thing. It makes for quite an expedited process. And quite a mess. First Evita, and now this one."

He sighed as he considered the unfortunate reality of the three violent human deaths.

"Quite a mess indeed."

"Speaking of mess," noted Terri, "We should clean up this one up. We don't need to draw any more attention to ourselves in this town."

"Of course, my dear. But let's be careful not to disturb the young ones. They have much work to do."

Three is as Magic as Can Be

Numbers are often used as a standard; a means to establish perspective. But can the same value represent both a standard of perfection and imperfection? For anyone who believes so, the very secret to happiness—and to madness—may reside in that one magic number.

The child had been living in his own filth for days. His parents were nowhere to be found. Two full cups of cold coffee sat on the kitchen table. They offered some proof that a family did indeed live here. But the splintered coffee table, shattered mirrors, and blood stains gave no reason to believe this was a home sweet home.

Detective Oswald Quinn stroked the young boy's filthy cheek and gave him a smile. He knew Child Protective Services would take care of the boy until his parents were found. But with each passing hour, that happy ending seemed less likely.

This wasn't the first of its kind. The Johnstown Police department and the FBI were no closer to discovering the whereabouts of any of the adults abducted throughout Cambria County than they were six months ago, when Oswald was called to the initial incident. That was four crime scenes ago. Ten adults—five sets of parents—were missing. Within each ravaged home, an only child was left alone.

Oswald watched as seven media teams descended onto the house. He hated the press. Their morbid questions from the other side of the yellow police tape disgusted him.

"The press is gonna go apeshit with this one," he turned and said to his partner. "Found—the youngest one yet to be left behind. Hey Taz, go over there and make sure none of them get a good shot of the kid when they bring him out. They don't need to exploit this shit. Better yet, grab a blanket for the social worker to put over him. That'll really piss 'em off."

Detective Patrick Taznowski, "Taz" to his fellow members of Johnstown's finest, had been Oswald's partner of 10 years. They shared a distaste for the press.

"I'm on it," Taz smirked.

Waiting until the last of the press had gotten their fill of suffering and depravity, Oswald and Taz cordoned off the main entrance of the house. It was only fifteen minutes to the station, but the Corner Coffee Shop was on the way. Once there, Taz slid his lanky frame into one of the restaurant's booths.

"Ya think I can get my caffeine in an IV drip? Today was fucking brutal. With any luck, some of the blood might turn out to be the perp's. There sure as hell was enough of it there today."

Oswald let out a growl and put up two fingers for the waitress. After ten years of regular patronage, hand signals usually sufficed for ordering.

"What are we missing, Oz?" continued Taz. "We have five families with the same socio-economic background. Five children left without parents, all under the age of ten. Each home shows signs of an ugly struggle."

"Nothing like what we saw today," Oz added.

"Right. A fucking mess. Yet we haven't even found a single piece of evidence to link *anyone* to these abductions. Not a clue. And so the press is making it look like we're not doing a goddamn thing."

With that, Taz pointed to the front page of the paper left behind on the abandoned booth next to theirs. The headline read:

POLICE REMAIN BAFFLED BY THE JOHNSTOWN PARENT-NAPPER

"Great, they gave the motherfucker a cute name now," barked Oz.

The dining room table was covered with a grimy 'Happy Birthday' table cloth, singed and stained with blood. Wearing a birthday hat and sitting at the head of the table, John Anthony was losing what he considered to be patience. His new parents seemed more interested in begging for their lives than in celebrating. But he would not be denied.

"No! Like this... Happy birthday to you... Happy birthday to you... Happy birthday dear Johnnyyyyy... Happy birthday to you. Stop and sing. Stop and Sing!"

John Anthony was trying to be nice this time. He wiped their bloodied faces clean and applied a fresh coat of lipstick to the mom's parched lips. He used the softest and smoothest rope he could find to bind their hands and feet. And he refrained from yelling or teasing; he was well aware of how painful that could be.

Despite his good behavior, this 40th birthday party wasn't turning out the way he had hoped. So far, these parents weren't any better than the others. They were, however, more vocal. Covering his ears, he roared his demands, hoping to silence them.

"Shut up. Shut up, shut up! Sing Happy Birthday!"

Mustering up what little courage he had, the male captive pleaded, "Please... we just want to see our son. He needs his parents."

His wife took a different approach.

"Fuck you, you ugly freak. What's wrong with you?"

What's wrong with you?

It was the one thing John Anthony hated to hear the most from any of his parents. What's wrong with you? The failure to love unconditionally always cut him to his soul. It always reminded him of the first parents. They asked that very same question, many times.

Whatever remaining patience he tried to display left the building. His mood changed immediately, and he grabbed the defiant mother by her matted hair.

"Nothing wrong with me!" he bellowed, seizing her head between his hands. A quick snap of the neck brought an end to the debate. He tossed her body onto the table, and watched as her head smashed the sickeningly sweet icing roses decorating the corner of the cake, snuffing out the candles.

"No. No. No! Three. Three makes a family!"

He looked toward the dad. Anger gave way to a sense of failure.

"It's always three."

He then snatched the cake knife from the table and plunged it into his remaining hostage's throat, thrusting it into his neck repeatedly until he had nearly severed his head.

He took a moment to catch his breath, and then wiped the sullied cake knife clean on the back of his victim's shirt. Taking his seat at the head of the table, he sliced a hunk of cake, relit the candles and made a wish.

Oswald sat down at the kitchen table, joined by a frozen dinner offering of Salisbury steak. His wife Connie had prepared dinner earlier, but only she and their son Dakota were around to eat it. More often than not, Oz was on his own for supper. Separate meals had become a common happening over the course of their 14-year marriage; just one turn on the pending journey toward separate lives.

The relationship became even more strained after their son Dakota showed up. Connie feared the life of a single parent. She felt that instigating fights with Oz over Dakota was her best shot at forcing his involvement in parenting.

For his part, Dakota began showing signs of emotional issues at an early age. He had always been an aggressive child. But, at the age of nine, he began growing excessively introverted and antisocial. Now a year older and preferring to go by "Cody", he offered little reason to believe this was just some phase he was going through.

Connie stood at the stove and lit a cigarette. "Nice to have you home before midnight. You did get my message that they suspended Cody from school today, didn't you? He's suspended for three days. He started a fire in the boy's room, Oz. I asked him why, and he refused to talk to me about it."

She took a long drag on her freshly lit cigarette and violently stubbed it out in the overflowing ash tray. But Oz knew she was imagining herself crushing it out on his forehead.

"Damn it, I can't do this by myself," she continued.

Oz put his fork down and rubbed his temples.

"I'll talk to him." Feeling he had zero chance of enjoying a peaceful moment until he followed through, he yelled for his son.

"Cody, get in here. We need to talk to you."

Cody trudged into the kitchen and fell into a seat across from his father.

"Cody, your mother tells me you were suspended from school for starting a fire in the boy's room. Did you do that?"

Cody looked at his feet and croaked out a simple "No." Oz shifted in his seat.

"Don't lie to us. Why the hell did you start a fire in the boy's room? What were you trying to prove? You could have been hurt. Or you could have hurt someone else. You could have burned the whole school down, for Christ's sake! Do you wanna go to jail like the criminals I see every day? Because that's what happens to arsonists."

Cody said nothing and stared at his sock-less feet.

"Answer me, Cody. What possessed you to pull such a stupid stunt?"

Cody shrugged his shoulders.

Livid, Oz slammed his fist on the table. "Damn it, Cody! What the hell is your problem?"

Unimpressed by his father's emotional outburst, Cody stood up from the table and popped in his ear buds for his mp3 player. Oz grabbed his son by the arm and threw him back in his chair. Tearing the ear buds from his ears, he threw the music player across the floor.

"There are children out there who have lost everything they've ever known. They've lost their parents. They've lost the people that love them the most in this world. You've got parents that care and love you, and this is how you treat us? Jesus, Cody. I'm a detective. I didn't raise you to be a monster."

Cody stared blankly at the floor. He showed no fear, no remorse, and no emotion.

While Oz continued squeezing Cody's arm, Connie had seen enough. She dug her nails into her husband's wrist.

"That's enough, Oz! Cody, go to your room. We'll talk about your grounding later." Oz released his grip, and Cody ran out of the kitchen.

"Well that went well, Dad. He's not one of your perps. He's our son."

"You told me to handle it. I handled it. What the hell do you want from me Connie? Ya know what? Fuck this shit, and fuck you. I'm going to bed. I gotta be at the station early tomorrow."

Oz threw the last few bites of his dinner in the garbage and headed toward the bedroom. Lighting another cigarette, his wife bellied up to the kitchen table and waited for her husband to fall asleep.

The cassette in the VCR recorder was crackling and warped from being rewound and played over and over again. The cartoon images on the television screen were blurred and jumpy, but John Anthony loved the songs and their messages. Especially the song *Magic As Can Be*. As it played, he sang along:

> *A guy loved a gal*
> *And birthed a tiny human*
> *Three is magic as can be*

As he sang, he felt a familiar excitement race through his body. Maybe this would be the time. He could have a mother and father. He could have a family this time. Why not now? This time there could be unconditional love, with no names like "ugly" or "freak." Mother, father, son. This time he could be part of a perfect family. All he had to do was find them.

It was approaching 4:30 PM when Oz's cell phone rang. It was Connie. A part of him wanted to ignore the call and let it go to voicemail, but that would be just prolonging the inevitable. Against his better judgment, he answered the phone. Connie was noticeably upset.

"Oz, we have a problem."

After making his way home, Oz found Cody sitting at the kitchen table. His face, arms and legs were swollen. His lip was split open. Connie had cleaned up most of the blood and had placed bags of frozen vegetables on his darkening bruises.

"Who would do this to him? Someone needs to pay for this. Oz, you'd better find out who did this!"

Oz knelt next to his battered child and gently patted his knee.

"What happened, Cody? Who did this to you?"

The boy sighed, "Some kids from school. I ran into them earlier. They were making fun of me for getting suspended. It's no big deal. They're just jerks."

Grabbing her cell phone, Connie pleaded, "Who are they, Cody? I'm calling their parents and we're pressing charges."

Cody jumped up, spilling a bag of mixed vegetables from his red thighs.

"No, you'll make it worse. Let it go, Mom. I'm fine."

"Both of you calm down" interjected Oz. "First, let's get you to the doctor and make sure you're...."

Cody cut him off. "I said I'm fine. I won't go. Nothing is broken. I don't need a doctor. Just leave me alone."

Throwing the frozen veggies to the floor, Cody ran towards his bedroom, slamming the door shut once he reached his destination. Oz followed and pounded on it.

"Open this door, Cody. Open it now!"

"Leave me the hell alone, Dad!" Cody yelled. "I said I'm fine."

Connie interjected, "Oz, let him be. I'll take care of him. I can call my sister to check him over. She'll be off from the hospital in a few hours. But you better find out who attacked our son. I will not have him being bullied like that."

"Damn it, Connie, Cody has gotta give me something to go on. I can't go after every frigging kid in the neighborhood.

For all we know, he instigated it. Let's not forget he just tried to burn the school down. He's not exactly a boy scout."

"So you've tried and prosecuted him already, huh? Maybe he's acting out, Oz. Maybe if your family meant more to you than your job, you would be right on top of this stuff."

Closing his eyes, Oz stood in front of his wife, vibrating from anger. He pointed a trembling finger in her face and opened his mouth to defend himself but nothing came out. Grabbing his keys from the kitchen table, Oz stormed through the house and slammed the front door so hard the walls shook.

John Anthony finished securing the ropes on his new parents. This abduction went smoother than the last. He learned it was best to knock mom out quickly with a blow to the head. Dad always put up a fight, but since this one was sleeping on the couch in a six-pack stupor, it was easy. He even had time to play with their other child. The first blow didn't completely knock mom out. Through mascara and blood, she begged him to leave the child alone.

John Anthony flashed back to his own youth. His mom had reprimanded him before for getting too close to other children:

"Johnny! How many times have I told you not to touch other kids? You're different from them, Johnny, and you gotta remember that. You might scare them. You might even hurt them. Last thing we need is a lawsuit on our hands."

The memory enraged him. He used a closed fist to silence this mom before she could say anything similar to him.

"Don't you look like shit?" Taz half-jokingly commented, handing his partner a cup of coffee.

"Do you really want to know?" Oz shot back with the look of a man who'd been beaten.

"No, not really, but you're gonna tell me eventually, so let's get it out of the way. What happened this time between late last night and the asscrack of dawn?" Taz tried to muster some interest, but most of his attention was devoted to the breakfast sandwich making its way toward his mouth.

"The kid got suspended from school. Connie is constantly on my ass to do more. Oh, and we have a case that needs my full attention. That's what happened."

Clasping his hand on Oz's shoulder, Taz sighed. "Brother, I have one thing to say: it sucks to be you."

Oz smirked, "Thanks for the empathy, partner. Since you're such a wealth of knowledge, is there anything from the lab yet?"

Taz rifled thru some phone messages left on his desk. "Nothing yet."

Oz opened the case file and scanned the photos for the tenth time this morning. "Yeah, day's getting better already."

John Anthony placed the squirming bodies of his parents on the floor in front of the television. He popped in his favorite tape and began to sing.

"Three is magic as can be. Oh yeah."

"Sing with me," he commanded.

He grabbed the mom's face. "Sing," he said, drenching her in spittle.

"I don't know the words," she sobbed.

"Listen to the song. Three is a family..."

Adrenaline had burned off most of his dad's buzz and he attempted to talk to John Anthony, man to man.

"We don't have a lot of money, but whatever you want, it's yours. Just don't hurt us."

John Anthony plopped down next to him and patted his head. "I don't want money. I want you to sing. Like this: A guy loved a gal and birthed a tiny human..."

John Anthony pointed to each of them and then to himself, "One, two, three. See? Three is magic as can be."

Trying to sound sincere through her terror, the mom's voice quivered, "Oh, so you want a family? But... my husband and I already have a family. We have a little girl at home who misses us."

John Anthony defiantly turned up the volume on the television to block out her unsavory statement, and pointed a sausage-like finger at each of them and counted out loud, "One, two, three. Three!"

The mom began to bawl uncontrollably.

"Please... I'm pregnant. Please let me go."

John Anthony froze. He never imagined his mom being pregnant. He stared out the window for several moments, like a computer processing too much data. He then pounded his head with his chunky palm.

"No, no, no, nooo! It's *three*."

He grabbed the mom by her restraints and slammed her up against the wall. Before she could plead for mercy, his fists raged—not to her face but to her stomach. The dad watched helplessly, able to only muster a whimper.

John Anthony pummeled her abdomen until her body hung limp. Her mouth gapped open, revealing a swollen and blood soaked tongue. Out of breath, Johnny dropped her spent carcass to the dirty floor and collapsed next to it.

It was a little late for visitors, which is why Oz was so startled by the 9:45 PM ring of the doorbell. Connie had gone to bed early. Oz was once again dining late, and alone. He trudged to the door, still working on the mouthful of toaster waffles he had prepared for himself. There, he was greeted by a middle-aged woman and her son, a few years older than Cody.

"Yes?" said Oz, swallowing as much waffle as he could in order to get the word out.

"Your son killed our cat," replied the agitated woman.

"I'm sorry, my son?"

The boy chimed in. "It's true. A couple of my friends and me, we saw him and we went over to stop it..."

"So you're one of the kids who beat my son up?" Oz interrupted.

The boy looked confused, "What? No... no way. None of us touched him. Nobody beat your kid up... but him. I mean, we wanted to hurt him. He killed my cat! But as soon as we confronted him, he freaked out. He started punching and scratching himself. He threw himself on the concrete and picked up rocks and smashed them into his legs. Sorry, sir, but your kid scared the hell out of us. We ran."

Oz recognized the look in the boy's eyes from many victims he'd interviewed over the years. It was genuine fear. Oz continued the discussion on the porch, promising he'd take care of the matter. But in reality, he had no idea what to do.

"This can't be. What the fuck is wrong with my kid?" he asked, to no one there. "Why the hell is my own kid such a fuck up? I gotta talk this bullshit out with Connie in the morning before I do anything; otherwise I'm liable to kill him. And of course, she's gonna chew my ass out. Son of a bitch... what is wrong with him?" He slammed his open palm against the siding. As if summoned by the force of his strike, it began to rain.

Cody watched and listened attentively from his bedroom window.

The next morning, Connie raced to the living room couch, where Oz had once more made camp for the night.

"Oz, he's gone. He's not in his bedroom. He didn't come down for breakfast. Did you see him at all this morning?"

Not quite awake, he mumbled, "What are you yelling about? What time is it?" Connie ignored him, continuing her room to room search for her son.

Taking her hunt outside, she yelled "Cody! Dakota! This isn't funny. Where are you?"

It took a moment for Oz to shake the stupor of the few hours of sleep he managed. His first reaction was that his son was up to no good again. Liar, arsonist, cat-killer, masochist. Now what? He considered stopping Connie long enough to share the news of last night's visitors, but he was exhausted and wasn't ready for that fight.

It wasn't until Oz canvassed the neighboring yards that the fear for his son's whereabouts roiled. Three blocks away, Oz found his son's Pittsburgh Steeler ball cap rolling in the street.

The sounds of Cody's escape from his bedroom window had been masked by the rhythm of the evenings' rainstorm on the flat roof. He had slipped out of his first story window many times before, always to return before his folks could discover his absence. This time, the thunderstorm added an extra rush. Moreover, this time he had no intention of coming back. He was a fuckup and he knew it. He had heard enough. He was an instigator, a troublemaker. Not exactly a boy scout. The reason for all the fights in their household.

Once he made his way out of the window, he proceeded on a journey into the unknown. As the son of a cop, he felt like he knew all about avoiding witnesses. He weaved in and out of alleys and dodged car lights, unsure exactly where he was headed. Despite the heavy clothing he had on, the rain stung his skin. The wind had earlier stolen his favorite hat, the only shelter his eyes had from the downpour. Cody knew he had to get out of the storm and figure out his next move.

Finding refuge would not be easy. It had been over a mile since he could rely on a street light for help. Only an occasional flash of lighting now provided any visibility. It was enough to see that there were no houses in sight.

The pavement turned into dirt, which turned into a walking path, which led into the thick of the Laurel Highlands state game land. The canopy of dense pine and oaks helped keep the rain at bay. At least now he felt he could hear himself think.

The woods were black, and walking was hazardous. Fallen trees, heavy underbrush, and large rocks littered his route. When the mud ripped a sneaker from his foot, Cody decided to take a moment to reevaluate his situation. He sat on what he hoped was a rotted tree stump and waited for the rain to let up. A crack of thunder made him jump to his feet, but the light display that followed gave his soggy feet wings. The silhouette of a small farmhouse appeared 200 feet in front of him, and then quickly disappeared into the darkness.

Cody rushed toward the house, making his way through the rotting door. To his surprise the house was warm. That helped assuage some of the horrid smell. He stripped off his jacket and threw it on the floor. He removed his orphan shoe and wrung out his socks on the weathered welcome mat. Without warning, a light flicked on in the kitchen, stealing his attention. Eclipsing the light was a man ambling towards him. Cody stood tall and puffed out his concave chest in hopes of intimidating his new roommate. Neither one moved. Eventually, it was Cody who decided to break the stare down.

"Why do you have that bandana wrapped around your head? Did you hurt yourself?"

John Anthony grinned. He knew by now how to scare other children away. He inched closer to Cody and removed his dirty bandana. Cody's eyes widened.

"Cool."

"Don't worry Oz, we'll find him."

Taz offered Oz an extra-large cup of coffee. Oz turned his head, uninterested in his partner's generosity. His hands fiddled with his son's ball cap.

"I know. Everyone is looking for him. I appreciate it. As a cop, you think you can at least protect your family. I never dreamed I'd be out searching for my own son. Connie and I really screwed him up, didn't we? Always fighting and...."

"Hey, lots of families fight," Taz interrupted. "Don't beat yourself up about that. Besides, it's tough being a kid. Especially being a cop's kid. He's just lashing out. But we'll bring him home and you'll work it out."

Oz nodded in patronized agreement.

"But you still need to beat his ass when he gets home, because wrong is wrong and you know damn well it'll make you feel better." Their moment of irreverent levity was interrupted from a message delivered by the chief himself. Another child was found.

Cody showed no fear. He quizzed John Anthony repeatedly about his face and about why he was in an abandoned house in the middle of the woods. John Anthony's reflexive notions to scare Cody away turned to unfamiliar feelings. It had been many years since his parents allowed him to play with other children.

Cody asked if there was a bathroom in the house. John Anthony, confused by the lack of fear Cody demonstrated, simply pointed to the closed door at the end of the hall.

"Thanks, I really gotta go," said Cody, and made his way.

As he approached the bathroom, the stench seemed to grow. He decided to take a detour, turning toward a side room. Feeling a switch by the frame of the door Cody took a chance that there'd be electricity and flipped it on. A dim overhead light bulb responded.

Cody's eyes grew and he let out a gasp. A pile of human remains littered the room. He swallowed deeply, covered his nose with his arm, and walked into the room.

His outstretched hand trembled as he endeavored to stroke the cool flesh of one of the dead. Cody knelt next to the body that he was attempting to touch. It was still warm and its tongue lolled from its mouth as if trying to tell him something.

Just as the man let out a soft grunt, John Anthony walked in and slammed the half-open door against the wall. Startled, Cody quickly turned. Just as quickly, he turned back to the body and pointed to the pile of bodies.

"This one's still alive."

The little girl was alive. A few bumps and bruises, but still alive. Knowing that Oz was preoccupied with his own problems, Taz took the lead on the scene. For his part, Oz struggled to calm his thoughts. He'd dealt with more than a few runaways in his day, and knew the odds of his son coming home on his own were good. But he also knew there was a serial killer on the loose.

Taz's cell phone rang, and he quickly answered it. He jotted something down in his notepad and slapped Oz excitedly on the back, "Oz, they found your boy. The kid turned on his cell phone. GPS got 'em. Let's get outta here and go bring him home."

The sun had gone down over an hour ago and the road stopped abruptly in the middle of dense acres of Pennsylvania state game land. Determined to find Cody, Oz and Taz broke out their flashlights and inched their way through the thick laurel bushes, trees, and brush.

The recent storms made the trek through the woods arduous. Any lingering doubts that Cody would be located were eliminated once they found his shoe drowning in the muck. That same muddy mess now proved to be an ally, leaving a trail of footprints toward an old farmhouse in the clearing. A flickering light from the front window gave them reason to hope Cody had made his way inside. As they approached the front door, they drew their weapons. Taz nodded to his partner, and Oz turned open the door.

"Cody? Cody, are you in here?" shouted a desperate Oz. As he made his way toward the lit room, Taz fell back and cautiously headed for the kitchen.

"Dad? Is that you?" Oz ran toward the sound of his son's voice. Cody met him halfway down the dark hallway.

The reunion lasted only seconds. They were soon joined by the massive shadow of John Anthony. Oz grabbed Cody and shielded him with his body, weapon pointed squarely at the figure in front of them.

"Who are you, and what are you doing here with my son?"

John Anthony tilted his head and stared down the barrel of the detective's gun. Like his staredown with Cody earlier, John Anthony simply stared in curiosity. But when Taz followed behind Oz, his curiosity turned to anger.

"No! There are too many people here!"

He charged Oz, taking two bullets to the shoulder before running into the darkened back rooms of the house. Before Taz could take a shot in the darkness, Cody stepped in the line of fire, shouting, "No! Don't!"

Taz sucked in a deep breath and lowered his weapon. "Jesus, what the hell are you thinking, boy?"

Oz ordered Taz to stick with Cody as he followed John Anthony into the darkness, with only a pocket flashlight to guide his way. The creak of a drawer opening took his pursuit to the kitchen.

Oz entered the room, and discovered a trail of blood leading around the corner. He followed it to a back hallway, which led to a bedroom. Before he could approach the doorway, John Anthony swung from behind the door, a large knife in hand.

Cody darted up the hall from the opposite end, with Taz giving chase.

"Cody, no, get down!" yelled Taz.

"Dad, stop!" screamed Cody as he desperately made his way toward John Anthony.

Both men's weapons were now aimed at the big man's head.

Cody stepped between his father and John Anthony. Cautiously, Oz inched his way towards his son.

"Cody, step out of the way. If he puts the knife down and turns himself in, no one will get hurt." Cody bristled at his father's orders.

"He's not gonna hurt me. He's a freak, just like me." Cody's words tore at Oz's heart.

"Cody, you're not a freak. No one thinks you're a freak. Now, please step out of the way." Cody backed himself closer to Johnny.

"I heard you last night. I've heard you and Mom talking. You don't know what to do with me. I'm a freak. I'm a fuckup."

"That's not true, Cody. Your mother and I love you."

"You were right last night, Dad. I'm the fucked up kid of a police detective who makes you look like shit."

Oz felt his hackles raise as well as his voice. "What the hell has this bastard done to you, Cody?"

"Nothing; you just hate people like me and him," said Cody, pointing over his shoulder to John Anthony. "We're freaks. Wanna see?" With that, Cody turned and faced the menace, and attempted to pull his bandana off. But in John Anthony's mind, Cody was planning to reveal the carnage he was hiding behind the bedroom door. In a defiant rage, John Anthony pushed Cody across the room, sending him crashing into Taz. Gunshots ripped through the fetid air, launching John Anthony backward through the rotting wood. Oz gagged at the smell emanating from the room, then kicked John Anthony's lifeless body as he cautiously surveyed the room. His heart sank. He knew what he was looking at. Taz grabbed a handkerchief from his pocket and held it to his mouth.

"Fuck. It was him."

Cody tried to approach John Anthony, but was intercepted by Oz, who attempted to hug his son.

"Cody, are you all right? Did he hurt you?"

Cody quietly shook his head, staring at John Anthony.

Kneeling besides John Anthony, Oz checked his pockets for identification and came up empty.

"Who the hell are you, ya murdering son of a bitch?" he muttered, removing the sweaty and stained bandana from his head.

"Jesus," Oz hissed, gasping at the deformed third eye socket in the middle of the killer's forehead.

Oz and Taz sat in Chief Brandon's office, joined by an inquisitive District Attorney Simmons.

"OK, so what do we know?"

"Well," started Chief Brandon, "we've identified the remains in the house. All of the missing have been accounted for. Each were bound and killed violently. We found one still alive, but he didn't last long."

"Poor bastard," chimed Taz.

"According to some evidence we've retrieved from the scene, our man goes by the name 'John Anthony Wilson'," the chief continued. "We have nothing on him, though. Neither does the FBI. Dental records and fingerprints turn up nothing. But the place was scattered with the belongings of Paul and Nancy Wilson, a cold case from Monaca. They were found murdered about 25 years ago. Neighbors at the time said they had a son, but MPD was never able to find any birth records indicating it.

"They said the kid was a loner; parents never let him out much and he wasn't allowed to play with the other neighborhood kids. Those who did see him described him as a big kid, messy, with a wrap... you know, one of those bandana things... on his head. He disappeared as a young adult; the neighbors seem to believe he ran away. No report was ever filed, though. He was the closest thing they ever had to a suspect. Only problem was, according to the records, he never existed."

The D.A. ran his fingers through his sparse hair. "The press is going to chew me a new one. We need more than this."

Oz hesitated, thoughts churning in his head. Apprehensively, he began to share them.

"Cody said he actually befriended this monster while he was being held prisoner."

"Stockholm Syndrome," added the chief. "Prisoners often relate to their captors."

"Right, right. But regardless, he was able to learn a little more. It seems the freak was obsessed with the number three. Kept playing some dumbass video from a kid's show with a song about it. I'm no head shrinker, but what if growing up in isolation, with parents that hid their freak kid in shame, you know... what if it sent him over? I think he wanted a different reality. To him, three meant perfection. The perfect family. Mom, dad, kid. Picket fence. Happy ever after. Blah blah."

"Makes sense" added Taz. "And Mom and Dad didn't play along. They hated him, or resented him, or whatever. He must've killed them over it. And then kept killing, in a hunt for his idea of perfection. The perfect family."

"That would be ironic," added the D.A.

"How so?" asked Oz.

"Ironic, that the number at the heart of his twisted dream was the real culprit here. Three made him imperfect, right? Personally, I think that's what sent him over the edge. Just think: if he hadn't been born with that freak third eye, maybe none of this would have happened. If not for that, maybe those bastard parents would have raised him properly, and he gets his perfect life after all. Maybe no insanity. Maybe no murders. Strange, no? The same number, exactly the perfect size for a family in his mind. But exactly one eye too many for someone craving to be normal. Perfection *and* imperfection. The difference must've driven him to an insanity we'll never understand."

"I have no interest in understanding that bastard," said Taz.

"It's something: how easily parents can fuck up their kids by making them feel imperfect," said Oz.

Cody and Oz sat in the living room playing video games. Oz was new to this, and it showed. He lost at every game they tried. It didn't seem to matter to either of them.

The whole ordeal of several months ago seemed to have a weird side effect. Oz took a desk job and was spending more time at home. He and Cody were closer than ever. There was no bickering, no fighting. Connie and Oz were happier than they had been in years. The family ate dinner together every night.

"I give up, you little monster," said Oz. "I'll never win. I'm going to bed."

"Hey! Don't call me that, Dad."

"You're right, I'm sorry. Just a little joke, buddy. I'm turning in though. I know it's a Saturday, but don't stay up all night playing these games, OK?"

Oz was up early the next morning. The desk job had him feeling sluggish, and he had recently started jogging in the mornings. It was still dark as he finished his last lap. He decided to make an impromptu stop for bagels.

"If I can get everyone else out of bed, we'll have a Sunday breakfast together," he told the cashier, who feigned some interest.

He made his way up the stairs to the bedroom. The early light of day was creeping through the window, providing just enough of a view to see that Connie was still sleeping. Oz walked around the foot of the bed to give her a Prince Charming-style wake-up kiss.

As he made his way around the other side, he noticed a pool of blood on the sheets. Quickly, he stripped them off and found Connie motionless. A large knife protruded from her abdomen. In her left hand was a stick from a pregnancy test; the result was 'positive'.

As he took the familiar trek out of the bedroom window, a sobbing Cody mumbled to himself.

"Three is magic as can be..."

Four Men on Horses

Many people believe that our existence as a species has been on a predetermined countdown since its beginning. But can the very shortcomings destined to lead humankind to destruction also prevent it? Has society outgrown its own death sentence? Maybe the answers lie in numbers, where almost anyone can lose the whole in the sum of the parts.

"I am Death! How can that tribe of putrid meat not fear me?" Death ranted, his voice accompanied by a thin hum of swarming bees as he sat at the round table hewn from the stump of charred Yew tree. His skeletal fist hammered its scorched surface as a horde of cadaver beetles scurried from the tattered sleeve of the Horseman next to him.

Flinching at his colleague's swift demise, Pestilence shouted, "Enough! Don't you think we are all enraged at the outcome of our failed Apocalypse? We are judgment. We are destruction. And God's precious beasts laugh in our faces!"

War pounded his paint splattered chest and grunted, "Those arrogant whelps! In ages past, they cowered at the sounds of our steed's hooves castrating their fouled ground. They hid their women and children. They hid their weapons, despite being the ones who cast the first stones."

Famine threw himself across the blackened table. His newly fattened belly protruded from his thin robes, almost threatening to burst. His plump arms stretched out reaching towards the clenched fist of Death.

"Listen brothers, I fear we are outcasts from our antiquity, pathetic relics to be shunned. Fear? They screamed in my face! Not begging for forgiveness. No, they screamed in my face and called me...called me..."

"What did they call you, brother?" demanded War. Famine closed his eyes, the sound of defeat clinging to the rasp in his voice.

"They called me...'dickhead'. Let me speak of my experience. But first, let me purge the bile and delicious fodder from my belly."

After taking a moment to collect his thoughts, Famine lay across the table as if submitting to a counseling session. He took a deep breath and began his tale:

"I rode into this trivial town in a rural area they have chosen to call "Ohio." I planned on slowly savoring the acrid taste of their suffering and their unmet desires from my parched lips. Once my ebony equine attempted to quench his never ending thirst in their rivers, the infection began to spread. I commanded the land to lay fallow and we watched the crops curl and shrivel. The water refused to satisfy stalk and fruit."

Famine gazed into a thick patch of trees, which served as a makeshift theater screen as the memories played out before his eyes while he recounted his tale. These were unfamiliar emotions to him, but he did his best to press on:

"I hid in the comfort of the shadows until I was certain the hunger had reached its unbearable zenith. It was then that I ventured into the fray. I came across a large filth-ridden hub of refuge. The garish sign screamed, "The Wall of Mart", or something equally senseless. I had waited so long to devour the weak that my insides began to eat themselves. So I advanced onto this Wall of Mart, and was enraged at the scene before me.

"Instead of wasting away from the lack of sustenance begot from their lands, the human roaches were fat and gorging themselves on an abundance of bread and meats. They were gleefully stuffing themselves with mass quantities of cream filled cakes and other pastries from within boxes. I touched the land and made it barren, but they were somehow not affected. I don't think they even noticed!"

"Nonsense!" replied Death. "What living creature fails to notice the hand of a Horseman?"

Undeterred, Famine continued reliving his personal horror.

"I buckled from the abhorrent hunger in my belly when a small group of female roaches surrounded me. But instead of fearing my existence, they spoke to me. They poked at my taut skin and questioned how they could get the same 'heroin chic' look as me. I know of no heroin chic look. What is heroin chic? They prattled on like preening yard fowl, quizzing me on my preference of diet pills and crampless laxatives. They asked which 'isle' my secrets could be located in. I assured them no isle on this planet was safe from my wrath. Yet they would not cease from speaking. I was almost driven mad by the senseless barrage of their asinine interrogation.

"I retreated into the night with what felt like only a fraction of my wits. I ambled towards another brightly lit dwelling, my horse drawn to its pungent stench. It was, in a word, obnoxious. I strode into the lodging and was quickly repulsed by the obese swarm of peasants hovering around vast rations of food as well as a bothersome clown taunting me to try a something called a "happy" meal. Intrigued by one particular bug's perverse fatness, I reached out and shoved my wasted finger into his thick, globular paunch. The pest dared speak back to me!"

"And what does one say when confronted by a Horseman of the Apocalypse?" asked Pestilence.

"The cockroach challenged me to a duel! All the while calling me 'frail', 'homeless' and...'dickhead'. I could have torn his plump limbs from his trunk, ending his misery and mine. But this Horseman never backs down from a duel when challenged. I admit it, I caved in to pride. I would suck down his fat soul and puke it back up just to prove a point. I... am... Famine."

Satisfied he had justified his response, Famine continued to recount his adventure:

"He and his ilk took great pleasure in preparing for the duel. I watched as they laid serving tray after serving tray littered with rations in front of us. Bemused, I needed clarity on the armaments of our duel. Where were the swords, the maces and axes for battle? I was growing weary of this duel and was tempted to end it myself by spewing a suffocating torrent of stomach acid and mucus. But just then, one of his tribe spoke.

'You have 10 minutes to eat as many burgers as you can,' he told me. 'The one that eats the most burgers is the winner. On your marks, get set, go!'

"It was a consumption contest I had consented to. I admit I was intrigued at the utter grotesqueness of the scene playing out in front of me as my rival ripped open steaming package after package, shoving the contents down his gullet. My eyes were enticed by his disgusting sin. A small part of me, though I hate to utter the words, was impressed. My portly dueling partner caught a whiff of my momentary weakness. His jaw muscles never stopped chewing as he chastised me as though I were unworthy of battle, saying, 'Better start eating there, Slim, or I am going to kick your anorexic ass.' The room exploded with cheers from the fat man's army. His words were foreign to me.

"Undaunted, I snatched one of the vile objects from the tray. I cautiously sniffed it, and recoiled at the stench. The crowd surrounding me began chanting, "Eat, Bones, eat! Eat, Bones, eat!

"It was then that my stomach let out a thunderous growl, silencing the raucous crowd. All eyes were on me. Turning my attention to the breathless and soulless quarry lying prostrate on a slice of bread, I allowed myself a taste. I am ashamed to say I found some primeval enjoyment in its flavor. I... I simply could not help myself. My eyes rolled back into their sockets as if I were in the throes of carnal ecstasy as the essence of this meat bathed my latent taste buds. In a ravenous spasm, I bit down on this meal of cattle they called a "burger." I nearly chomped on my own finger, I tell you. Globs of some blood-like substance gushed down my chin. I felt as though I was eating something or someone freshly killed in battle, its heart still pumping.

"The restaurant erupted with the same rousing chant, 'Eat, Bones, Eat. Eat, Bones, Eat.' Like one of Death's prized hell hounds, I ripped into these burgers, devouring them one after another. Within minutes I had consumed at least 24 of them, including their greasy paper wrappings.

"My opponent showed no sign of slowing down, but his eyes reflected the burden of a man who had met his match. Amid the rowdy chanting someone stood on one of the tables and announced, 'Sixty seconds!' As my adversary squeezed his eyes shut and concentrated on his next torturous bite, I changed my strategy. With two burgers clenched in my fists, I quickly cracked both sides of my jaw, causing the bone to pop and unhinge, thus making it easier to take in two burgers at once.

"A countdown began. The crowd was deafening as the remaining hamburgers were counted. Once again the room grew silent. The timekeeper minion took his spot back on the table.

"He began to announce the results of the contest. My opponent—who went by the name "Stu-Man the Punisher," had consumed 34 of these burgers in the allotted ten minutes. I had consumed 32. The Punisher was declared the victor!

"The throng of observers exploded with shouts, whistles and hearty slaps on the back. I, meanwhile, lolled in the rigid plastic seats, my concave stomach now bloated and pregnant with these burgers. The one known as 'The Punisher' pushed his way towards me.

"'Not too bad Slim, but you still lost,' was his boast as he turned to join his comrades.

"'Oh, I almost forgot,' he declared, and with a right cross, the peasant struck me in my already dislocated jaw.

"'You never fuck with the Punisher,' was his final warning to me. I could do nothing, having been put into some sort of paralysis by the food I had ingested."

"So, that is why you look like a fattened calf?" asked Death. "I assumed it was from devouring the souls of the feeble after an epic battle. Never would I have thought the battle would devour you." Death's fingers clacked together like a wind chime as he nervously wrung his bony hands.

"I tainted the water," Famine bemoaned. "I poisoned field after field. And yet, the human filth grew heavy on food transported in metal beasts from lands elsewhere. They made a mockery of me, challenging me to a duel from which I could not back down. How was I to know the challenge would be so... delicious? I have failed you, my brothers."

With that, Famine slumped in his seat at the round table, patting his corpulent belly.

"We must find this scourge Stu-Man the Punisher and bring him to justice," War declared. "Let me take care of him, brother. I promise I will crack open the pus-filled meat sack and dance in his blood." He postured as he raised his green, pink and yellow-smattered battle mace which perfectly matched the stains on his armor.

"By the odd appearance of your weaponry," Famine quipped, "it seems your visit through the ether also failed to find bloodshed and carnage." His laughter caused him to pass gas, creating a rumble from his seat beneath him. Pestilence snickered and waved the foul gas towards him. He took a deep breath, filling his lungs with his brother's noxious fumes.

"An intoxicating aroma," he said, fanning any lingering stink all over his body like an exotic perfume.

Disgusted, War slammed his mace on the ancient yew table. It failed to leave a mark. "Damn it, brothers! I am ashamed to say the humans bested me, so I won't! But I will discuss my venture with all the bravado my valiant self can muster."

Like Famine before him, War struggled to reveal his tale. None of these four were accustomed to discussing failure, but War in particular despised anything but conquest.

Begrudgingly, he began to share the horrors of his own encounter:

"I rode for days, searching for the perfect location to sow the seeds of Armageddon. The spot was a village named Gettysburg, in a region referred to as Pennsylvania. The battlefields and surrounding acreages that hosted the Civil War were soaked in the gore of thousands of soldiers and innocents. The lingering spoor of battle was heady. I filled my lungs with the aberrant energy.

"The field I followed butted up to a few small dwellings. The familiar rallying of combat stoked my attention. From a short distance, I could see a heartening sight: a small group of young boys thumping their chests, displaying their verve in an amateur pissing contest. In the middle of the melee were two equally matched youths with their hackles standing at the ready, their supporting sides just as divided.

"Reveling in the moment, I watched the boys as they exchanged unintelligible insults and threw reckless, unskilled fists in the air. One boy's weak punch connected with the other boy's head. Grabbing a fistful of hair, he started pulling. The second boy wasted no time securing a handful of the lucky boy's mop and yanked. Both boys tugged at each other's sweaty mane, not completely certain what they were trying to accomplish.

"I watched, bewildered and a little mortified at the boy's ineffective style of combat. Hair-pulling is not a respectable battle move, even for naïve warriors. Finally I could no longer hide in the shadows and watch the awkward melee. With mace in hand, I trotted in on my equine monstrosity, knowing the very sight of its skinless body and exposed musculature would divulge its rider's infamy to the youth persevering in this pitiful bout. As I dismounted my flayed steed, I was greeted by gasps."

Famine, Pestilence and Death grinned. The thought of mortals gasping in horror at their sight had been something they had looked forward to for many centuries.

"I hope you taught them how to die like warriors," said Death.

"I tried. As I approached them, I snarled, 'What manner of combat is this? No fighter, no matter how green, would use hair-pulling to secure their enemy! That is skirmish best left to the fairer sex.'"

As his comrades erupted in laughter, War continued his tale:

"It was then that one of the lads scoffed at me. 'What amuses you, little ant?' I demanded. The boy laughed even harder, causing the rest of the youthful flock to breakout into hysterical laugher. But no one answered me. I grew impatient as the laughter continued. One unusually tiny boy tugged on my cape.

"The child cupped his mouth with his hand and whispered, 'You said sex,' inciting a second round of raucous laughter.

"'Enough!' I bellowed as I eyeballed each child, inciting an effective dose of fear before continuing my reprimand.

"'This domain has made you soft, little maggots. If you are going to die proudly during this Apocalypse, you must learn how to fight. Pick up those sticks. Be honored as I, the Horseman of War, shall reveal the mysteries of how to battle like a god... and consequently, how you shall die like men.'

"Unable to move from terror, the boys stood staring as I wielded my mace, pointing it at the original two scrappers. I demanded that they pick up their sticks and defend themselves. 'One of you will die honorably at the other's hand. A stick, although a crude instrument, can easily break limbs and burst yielding brains from their skulls. Take hold of the stick like this...'

"Suddenly, my demonstration was interrupted by a whimper and then a sniffle. These turned into a deluge of bawling and tears. One of the boys threw himself on the grass and wailed for his mother!

"I commanded them to cease their sorrowful noise, or I would rip their tiny tongues from their heads and feed them to my horse. I promised to give them a reason to cry out. But this did little to quell the children's cries. Their howling rang through the air, calling the attention of more than a few protective mothers who recognized the sounds of their wounded cubs. They descended on me like a voracious lion on a gladiator.

"Like a cursed viper, one female hissed, 'Just who in the hell do you think you are?'

"I beat my chest and proclaimed 'Woman, I am War!'

"The din of my reputation fell on fatuous ears as another woman, just as dim, cackled, "What the hell did you do to my child?" and called me a *per*-vert. She threatened me with some pitiful state of human authority and had the gall to intimidate me by debasing the very parcel that houses my seed!

"I was flanked by the onslaught of enraged women as they shouted, cursed and flung bewildering insults at me. Suddenly, one of the mothers charged, dousing me with a faceful of some vile mist. I later learned this weapon is known by the locals as 'pepper spray'. I growled and clawed at my face, fighting the invisible invader assaulting my eyes. As I staggered backwards I tripped on a confound rock and fell. While I was down, a second mother seized the opportunity to attack me with another weapon, which shot the power of lightning to my buttocks. I writhed as the electrical shock forced my muscles to spasm and shiver."

War's apocalyptic brothers howled in laughter. "Bested by females?" laughed Death. "Suddenly my failures seem insignificant!"

"These female warriors were armed with weapons that I had no knowledge of!"

"So you ran?" asked Pestilence. "You could not swat the female gnats away, so you ran from them?"

"Sensing trauma, my horse saddled up next to my quaking body and collapsed next to me. Understanding his intentions, I laced my fingers around his bridle and gave it a heave. The horse rose, pulling me to my feet, and thus I was able to make a hasty retreat. The mothers were left with their scared children, waiting petulantly for their salvation to arrive in a barrage of metal beasts screaming bloody hell."

"Quite the battle," bemused Famine. "The End Days are not supposed to bring your end."

Ego destroyed, War hesitated but continued his recant.

"With regret, there is more..."

"Once I secured my bearings and shook off the electrifying jolt, anger swelled within me. I raised my mace to the sky, let out an ear-splitting roar, and spat on the ground. My steed kicked up the soft dirt with his hooves and snorted in accord with my ire. It was then I noticed two teenagers gawking from a few yards away. I decided I would not treat these young ones with the same pity I had for the earlier band. I reared my horse, expecting them to scuttle like human roaches. But instead they inched closer, their mouths hanging open. They pointed communications devices at me, recording my image with smiles on their faces. One of the teens uttered, 'Dude. This is awesome!'

"I poked the teen in the chest with my mace. 'How dare you speak in the presence of War!' I shouted. The other boy spoke up. He explained that they were warriors as well, and invited me to join them in combat. This was finally what I had hoped for. I could feel the blood lust raging through my very being. After all, my purpose is to wage war, and these earth-bound bastards were willing to take me into combat. I could begin culling the wounded and once the fair, weak and lame were eradicated, I could harvest the skin and bone of the most robust."

"The first young warrior spoke. 'Come on man. The games are about to begin.'

"With bared teeth I replied, 'Yes, impetuous one. Take me to your battle grounds. Let the games begin.'

"Our arrival into the battle was made through a wooded clearing and met with little fanfare. But for a few armed soldiers, the combat arena was void of souls to shred. One of the warriors, who called himself 'Braydon', gathered the small ops together to discuss strategy. He directed his men to, 'Hit em hard and hit em fast.'

"I was compelled to interrupt this speech with a hearty snort. 'Is that a call to arms, boy? Pathetic. If you want to rally your troops and prepare them for carnage you must speak to them like this...'We shall crush the enemy's heads under our boots and rip out their throats as they cling to their last dying breath. We shall pile their shredded corpses in a heap and dance naked on their limbs. We will claim our victory with blood-stained flags planted firmly in their stinking orifices.'

"The troops were oddly quiet. Finally, Braydon broke the silence. Sputtering the ineloquent words, 'Yeah, what he said. Let's kick some ass... fuckers!' The soldiers gave a sincere battle cry and quickly ran for cover, leaving me in the clearing.

"Finally engaged in battle, I felt rejuvenated from my earlier defeat. I prepared for the sweet butchery of souls, when Braydon's voice echoed from somewhere within earshot.

"'*Now!*'

"The sound of hundreds of rounds of ammunition buzzed through the air, hammering me with throbbing pellets that exploded in florescent hues. My red—and now yellow, blue and pink—horse thrashed and bucked as these balls of ink stained us. After a full thirty seconds, the hail of gunfire ceased.

"'What is the meaning of this, you insolent nurslings?' I asked. 'I am War. I will split your weak spines in half. I will rend your eyeballs from their sockets...'

"It was then that Braydon, still referring to me as 'dude', informed me that I could not retaliate.

"'Sorry, but you've been hit, like a million times so you're out. You gotta go to the deadbox with the rest of the dead.'

"'I will destroy all of you!' I assured. Once again I reared my dye-stained horse, my mace at the ready. The camouflaged warriors took aim and fired round after round of their vibrant ammunition, splattering me as though I were their canvas. I charged through the clearing, racing past my hidden attackers as they pelted what they could of my dust. Breaching a hole with my mace through a standing of trees, I hurdled the opening and escaped into the ether."

"So you understand my brother," said Famine. "The humans are a shrewd race. They even bested the mighty War!" With this, Famine released a vulgar belch.

"Bite your tongue, Famine, unless in your gluttonous state you've already eaten it. There will be retribution! I will slake my thirst by bathing in the human's blood."

Pestilence chimed in. "Brother War, it looks as if you have already been bathed in the blood of a slaughtered jester."

War simply growled at him. Death seemed to be smiling, enjoying the levity on War's behalf, although no one could be sure since Death's skull was devoid of facial muscles and lips. Instead of continuing to poke the angry bear, Death turned his attention to Pestilence, who was furiously scratching his nether-region and investigating the myriad of insects adhering to his slight frame. They scurried and darted under his robe as if he were transforming into another sordid creature. Death slipped a skeletal finger under Pestilence's robe and spoke in nothing more than a whisper.

"And what have we here, brother? What makes your skin reject your infestation and has you clawing at your organ? Speak to us Pestilence. Better yet, show us. There are only your brothers present."

Pestilence slapped Death's invading finger, preventing him from further exploration under his robe.

"It is none of your concern, brother. As Famine has affirmed, these humans are a shrewd race, a curious race, a hearty race. Not the race we once knew."

As he spoke, he reflected a twinge of sadness and raked his groin with his fingers in such a fervor that insects sprang from his robe, bouncing off War's splattered armor, vaulting through Death's eye sockets and landing on Famine's swollen belly. Snatching a plump beetle from off his gut, Famine gave it a sniff and stuffed it in his mouth.

"I have shared my awkward tale, as has War," said Famine. "So speak, brother, before I get weak from lack of sustenance and decide I no longer care."

Pestilence hung his head, "I am not proud." With this, he began his own tale:

"My ordeal began in the influential kingdom of this land dubbed 'America', Washington D.C. As I approached, the roadways were congested with metal chariots. The angry-sounding metal creatures swallowed up most of the thoroughfares and pathways, preventing me from spreading infection as I rode within the chaos on a hoary spray of insects and contagion in the sculpt of a horse. I gawked at the multitude of pedestrians walking small footpaths, and peered into automobile windows as they inched by, delighted to see a vast quantity of people inhabiting the area. It would be the ideal killing ground.

"The air near the Lincoln Reflecting Pool was almost wintery on this day. It seems I had arrived on a holiday, All Hallows' Eve. The area was lively, with large touring groups and locals unwinding, celebrating the holiday in various forms of costume. I inhaled the cool breeze, picking up the scent of individuals in various forms of decay and disease. However, an unfamiliar medicinal scent wafted from body after costumed body. It made my nose burn. Attempting to blow the stink from my nostrils, I fired a slew of maggots onto the cape of a diminutive vampire. In return I was flipped a middle finger, and the child ran to his mother.

"A small crowd of teenagers retrieved their communication devices to capture my image. They seemed to assume our godly forms as elaborate costumes. Fools. I issued hushed commands to my horse, which reared on its hind legs and leapt into the reflecting pond. As he sunk to the bottom, the crowd that had gathered stood pie-eyed. A few gasped in trepidation waiting for the horse to surface and return to me.

"I did not keep them waiting long. The water began to bubble and roil as if it were a massive soup pot. The ground along the pool rumbled, creating a low, jaw-quaking buzz. But instead of the spectators retreating in fear as they should have, they inched closer to the water's edge!

"As the low hum reached an echoing crescendo, a geyser of droning insects emerged from the memorial pool. They hovered above the water, awaiting direction from me. On my command, the thick potage of bugs scattered throughout the rally of bystanders. The humans began anxiously swatting the insects as they landed in their hair, coats and costumes."

"Finally!" cheered Death, "we have a tale of success. How many died at your hand, brother?"

Pestilence ignored the question and continued his story:

"As my minions attacked, the crowd simply ignored them. They were more interested in me! They swarmed me much in the way my little minions had attempted to swarm them. They asked friends to capture images of them standing next to me. They posed, with various finger gestures. One woman shoved her newborn son in my arms while another asked me to carve my name in her ample bosom.

"I called out to my insects. I craved a taste of what they sampled in the human meat sacks. I opened my mouth, inhaling the insects and their knowledge. But they were unaffected by my maladies. How was it possible? What raced through their feeble bodies to keep them from dying? Angered, I unleashed even more, some of the most vile, disease-carrying creatures at my disposal.

"That is when the metal black birds arrived, creatures of this kingdom's military. The thunderous sound and wind of these creatures caused the crowd to shield their faces, yet they continued to attempt to capture images of the events.

"A voice emanated from one of the metal creatures. 'Everyone, stand back from the pool. We will be releasing the spray on the count of three, starting now, one...'

"People scattered for cover. The air of the thin October veil hanging above the water was fouled with a pernicious smog, immediately exterminating all of my insects. The once buzzing haze dropped one by one into the pool, their dead bodies blemishing the surface of the water. The vile cretins obliterated my damned horse!

"Once the threat to the people of this kingdom was eradicated, the metal beasts swiftly retreated, leaving me to stand vigil over the thousands of insect corpses now afloat on the water, my obedient steed. I fell to my knees, completely defeated in mere minutes. My disgusting weakness garnered the impudence of a young male who approached me in a daft space traveler suit. Foolishly, he laid a hand on my shoulder and spoke what I grasped as intimidations in my ear.

"'Hey big guy,' he uttered. 'Sorry about your bugs. They were cool as hell. The Man had no right to fuck em up like that.'

"The nerve of that pissant.

"I grabbed the spaceman by his silver lame poncho and lifted him off his feet, demanding to know how he and his kind came to be immune to so many diseases. I was told of an army... he called their fortress the 'Center for Disease Control.' There, they wage a battle against disease. Eradicating polio, smallpox and..."

Pestilence's eyes filled with tears.

"...the bubonic plague! My finest work."

"I released the spaceman from my grip, and he looked upon me with pity as he scurried off. *Pity!*

"In anger, I smashed my fists to the ground, calling up a million black widow spiders. This caught the attention of a lone female, costumed as one of the walking dead. She had failed to evacuate the area as the military had ordered. Instead, she approached me.

"She introduced herself as Lynne. She carried the same medicinal scent I had smelled before on all the other humans, yet hers was somehow different. It was acrid, penetrating and tainted. It was beautiful! I grabbed her stringy blonde hair, wrenching her from her knees onto the ground and shoved my nose into the crook of her faux-zombified neck. The stench exhilarated me. I inhaled even more deeply as I followed her neck to her hair, and then she struck me!"

"Please brother, tell me you killed at least this one mortal?" queried Death.

Aye, I prepared to slay her with my bare hands. But she proceeded to ask me if I wanted to 'get high'. She raked her ragged finger nails down my chest to the leather cord synching my robe. She asked if I had anything.

"'What do you speak of, woman? What is it you have the mettle to ask of Pestilence?' I demanded."

"I see now," laughed Death. "You took this female, didn't you?"

"You don't understand," continued Pestilence. "She actually *wanted* to be taken. I typically find such things to be vile. But this one... was different. She was handsome with her sickly pallor and bruised skin. She looked and reeked of death and it was desirable. It has been many hundreds of centuries since I... and so I... I..."

"You took her body," said Death.

"And I was quickly reminded why such things are reserved for their shattered corpses. My god-like enthusiasm broke her like a child's toy. But I must shamefully admit... I liked it. Until the incessant itching started. My groin soon burned not from the fire of a zealous tryst but of an alien infestation! The prickling intensified. I felt as if I would rip my manhood from my body. The insects harbored in my flesh were wriggling away from their warm, moist haven, many leaping off me, usurped by a foreign colony of bugs and disease. Unable to satisfy my maddening itch, I called for my steed to return, but his slaughtered remains were now a feast for the birds. Defeated and apparently infected with an unknown assailant, I called upon the haze and walked through the ether alone. My failure is complete."

War tumbled off his seat in a fit of wild laughter as Pestilence recounted his visit. Famine was on his knees attempting to catch his breath between hysterics and gurgled belches.

Raising his left fist in the air (his right was busy clawing at his groin), Pestilence shook it at his insolent brothers.

"I have shared my plight and you mock me? You should spend your time pondering this new spawn of human scum and how they..."

Death lazily interrupted, "...brew a sexually transmitted disease that revolts the very crickets and crabs born of Pestilence's prick? Yes. That is a subject that interests us all. Nonetheless, it is quite humorous."

"Well, Death, you have heard each of our apocalypse commencing tragedies. What of yours? You sit here so smug and judge us. What of your cold, silent calculations?" Pestilence sneered, shifting in his seat, visibly struggling not to touch himself.

Folding his bony arms across his exposed breast bone, Death reclined in his chair and whispered, "It is not pretty. But it should have been."

Apprehensively, Death began to tell of his plight:

"My pale horse demanded a reprieve from any further resurrections. Content in the primordial soup, the equine declined my latest invitation to carry me into an Apocalypse. Forced to transport through the ether unaided, I assessed my battle field options and chose my destination by reputation. I would begin in the village named Murder City USA, New Orleans.

"The streets were littered with trash of all colors, creeds and ethnicities. Women and young men peddling their flesh as vulgar displays of drunkenness. Gluttony and acts of violence ravaged the city. Baptized in the torrent rainwaters of the occult, New Orleans used blood sacrifice as a storefront for tourists, marketing death. This was by all accounts a town I could have become enamored with.

"An extraordinary gothic stone and iron building piqued my attention, as did the filthy marquee: 'Club Hades.' I entered through its heavy wooden doors and was greeted by a group of pale women sipping drinks in skull-shaped glasses. They queried me with such questions as: 'Is that a mask or a prosthetic?', and 'Were you here last week dressed like Nosferatu?'

"Someone dubbed 'DJ' created thunderous music, causing my skull and teeth to rattle against each other. The room was packed with mortals in all manner of macabre clothing. It was peculiar, yet strangely inviting.

"A young man costumed to look like a vampire stopped to compliment me, telling me I passed for a believable Reaper. As I attempted to explain that I am indeed *the* Reaper, the man mocked me! Angered, I ceased the music with a snap of my fingers and lifted the bastard human with my hand, dangling him over the crowd. This caught the attention of the ants, who soon stopped to gaze upon the sight. So I gave them a real sight to see.

"Another flick of my fingers saw the doors lock, and I commanded the flames from the hundreds of candles and torches strewn about to rise. I announced my intentions.

"'Human sludge. This is the end of days, *your* days. I am the monster under your bed. I am the killer among killers. I am the devourer of souls. I am Death.'"

"Tell me that you smote the entire crowd," pleaded Pestilence, almost in jest. "Tell us all of the final victory of Death over life." The group knew at this point that Death's story would end no better than the three before it.

"If but I could, my brothers. But as you have already learned, the mortals are different. It is as if they care for nothing.

Death continued his story:

"My tirade was met with initial silence, which I hoped was fear. But instead, the silence was swallowed up by mass applause bouncing from stone wall to stone wall. Confused, I dropped my would-be victim. The boy's left leg snapped as he fell to the black marble floor. But instead of begging for mercy, this insect crawled to the hem of my robe and cried, 'Take me! Take me first! I would be honored.' Honored! His pleas drew many other declarations of reverence, homage and self-sacrifice as well. Soon the polished floor at my feet was teeming with warm bodies, each waiting for a chance to touch me. The group of females I met on my entrance into this place now tore off their shirts and pleather corsets, exposing their sweaty breasts in an attempt to gain my favor.

"I made my way to the station where the vagrant named DJ held court, playing the vile music and speaking to the masses with the use of some amplification device. I used this to speak to the crowd. 'You are imploring me to let you taste your mortality? Where is your fear?' I asked.

"A man dressed in Victorian period clothes, aviator goggles and a tinfoil codpiece spoke up, saying that they have been waiting for me; waiting for me to cleanse the world."

"The Lord of Death", laughed War, "reduced to being the world's soap!"
Undeterred, Death continued:

"Another spoke, grabbing a toy displayed from behind the bar and presenting it to me. 'You are a hero in this culture,' he said. 'See, we even have action figures that revere you. I know this is a long shot, but would you sign my numbered Dead Dolls of the Apocalypse?'

"I tell you, my brothers, they mock us with playthings! We are no more menacing to them than those children's toys of theirs! I was even asked to assign my name on a female's ass next to someone named 'Gene Simmons.'"
"Why not just smite them all where they stand?" asked War. "Why continue to allow this nonsense?"
"As sure as I stand before you now, I tried," bemoaned Death. "The throng was strong; their worship of me was overwhelming."
With what little remaining pride he could muster, Death resumed his tale:

"The human playing the music summoned a tune christened, 'Don't Fear the Reaper'. The crowd cheered and gyrated to the music while I stood bewildered. I could not even lift an arm, as this crowd engulfed me as though I was a morsel of food, and they a hungry pack of wolves. They forced me to a station where libations of alcohol were being served, and began demanding that I partake of it with them. For the first time in many centuries, I felt like... I belonged.
"A heavy-set female with black fairy wings and a face tattoo tugged at me to join her in an area called the 'dance floor'. The alcohol... the beat of this strange music... my bones began to shake and quiver. I was 'possessed' by the music and I regret to say...I liked it. I began to speak to these people, who

viewed themselves as my followers. I posed for images with them. I told them stories no mortal has ever heard. I was actually having fun, without carnage and destruction."

"*Fun?*" exclaimed Pestilence. "We have been charged with bringing in the End Days... the final destruction of mankind. And you speak of fun?"

"I am not proud of my failure," replied Death. "But let me remind you that I am not alone in it."

His message clearly conveyed to his brothers in arms, Death continued:

"Sometime after midnight, the mortal charged with providing the music announced another arrival. A jester or performer of some sort, named DJ E-VUL Dead. The crowd erupted in applause as this vagrant made his way onto a platform to perform his craft. All eyes were upon him. Like a mischief of rats, they scurried from my side and charged the mount from which he did his work, undulating and swaying to the hypnotic beats.

"It was then that I realized... I had succumbed to ego and pride. I was jealous! How could they abandon me so quickly? I am the Horseman, The Reaper! I am Death and the people had loved me mere minutes ago. If they were so impressed by my prowess before, I figured a demonstration would return them to the fold. So I began to take the life from my competition, bringing the E-VUL Dead to a painful spasm on the floor. My followers gazed upon his writhing body, and then turned their attention toward me. Their words were not those of endearment.

"'Awww... Death, this is not cool.'

"'At least let him finish the song.'

"'If he's dead his music will just explode on the charts! He'll be famous.'

"The thought of giving my adversary more popularity from his demise vexed me. These were *my* worshippers, my flock, my lambs to slaughter as and *if* I wished. How dare this insignificant mortal steal them away?

"The tattooed wench with the black wings begged me to release him, as she was enjoying his musings and wanted them to continue. The entire flock watched for my next move. With all eyeballs on me, I waved my hand and released the desperate human from my invisible grip. Once his face shifted from blue to pink, this E-VUL DEAD coughed a few times and continued his muse. Like rats trailing the piper, the crowd followed him. Alone, I consumed several vats of alcoholic drink and made my exit into the inviting arms of the ether."

Pestilence shook his withered head. "You are getting soft, Death, enamored with humans! Maybe you should keep them as your little pets."

Death cracked his bony knuckles and hissed his reply.

"Speaking of little pets, how's your manhood? Have you scratched yours off yet?"

"At least there is manhood between my legs! Unlike you, skeleton. Pleasures of the flesh are lost on you."

Death lunged at Pestilence. Snapping Death up by his hood, War squelched the tantrum, tossing him into his seat; his bones awarded a sickening crunch.

Famine chimed in, "Brothers, you quarrel like children. Your failures demonstrate your frailties, and your reactions only serve to magnify them."

"Our failures," exclaimed Death. "And what of yours, you fattened calf? I shall cut open your newfound girth and let the hell hounds consume it!"

A melee erupted among the four, with all engaged in argument and shoving. It was then that a familiar voice echoed over the riot.

"Why have you failed me?"

The four froze in fear, each assuming a look as though they were a child caught in mischief by a parent. They said nothing.

The voice repeated the query.

"Why have you failed me?"

Famine spoke, apprehensively. "This world... it seems to have simply outgrown us! They do not respect what we represent. They do not fear us! Mankind has changed since we took this charge, eons ago." The others nodded in fearful silence.

"We are to bring the Apocalypse to the world and yet one by one, each one of us failed. The human race has outwitted us and worse, they do not fear us."

After a moment of uneasy silence, the voice returned.

"And this takes you by surprise?"

The four looked at each other, but none was able to muster the nerve to reply.

"It has been this way from the beginning times. Mankind changes. Knowledge grows. Each generation is fueled by the actions of the previous. This is by design. Their boldness, their self-assurance, their confidence. All by design."

The four remained silent, listening intently despite not understanding.

"Your failure is not a matter of underestimating your prey."

The group continued to look at each other. None dared speak up.

"Your failure is one of strategy."

War raised an eyebrow. He of all knew of strategy. Yet he remained dumbfounded.

"Since the dawn of time, you have been charged with one mission. Together, you are to bring about the End Days. Together. There is no strength in individualism. Individualism breeds ego and weakness. Alone, your status made you believe you were gods among minions. Alone, you were assimilated into the group. You took their weaknesses and failures as your own.

"*This* is why you failed."

War spoke, albeit cautiously. "I understand now. Only together, only as four, can we succeed. *The* Four. The Four Horsemen." Looking to his brethren, he proclaimed "We shall not fail again!"

Extending his massive, paint-stained arms, War explained, "Look at me, splattered with humiliation. And you Famine, plumped by deceit. Pestilence has been overpowered by seduction and Death, deluded by vanity. We were defeated not by the human roaches, but by ourselves. To win this crusade, we must unite. We are strongest together and weakest apart. So brothers, do you now understand the battle plan?"

Pestilence slammed his fist on the charred yew table, scattering insects in all directions. "I do not enjoy admitting when you are right, brother, but I understand. We shall revisit the earth and decimate humanity together."

Death agreed, "Yes. It is the dawning. I am ashamed I was outdone by my vanity, but it has fueled my bloodlust. They want to know Death? They shall know the cruelty and sadistic nature of Death."

Brandishing his trusty mace, War roared, "It is settled. Mount your steeds. We shall ride through the ether together and conquer what we could not conquer before and it will be savage, bloody and glorious! We are the Four Horsemen. Together, we are the Apocalypse."

"Brothers, I have but one request," urged Famine. "Such a daunting task cannot be met with hunger. Let us begin by stopping for some of these 'burgers.' With our bellies full, we shall have the strength to overcome. And should I encounter that fat bastard Stu-man, I shall not fail in his contest again."

"Nor I," proclaimed War. "I shall return and show these young warriors how to battle. The championship will be mine!"

"Right you are, brother," proclaimed Pestilence. "And I shall return to the kingdom of D.C. and unleash a suffering mankind has never seen. I will use my fame to spread this itch to every wench I encounter, enjoying their flesh and spreading my plague."

"Aye" said Death, "and I will ride to New Orleans, where I will replace this E-VUL and become the NEW master of musical charm. All shall dance before me!!"

"Let us ride!!" said War, as the four rode off into the ether.

The four disappeared in the dust kicked up by their charging steeds. As they faded, a somber quiet slowly replaced the echoes of their bravado.

"End of days, my ass," sighed the voice.

May Day Number Five

Numbers drive our methods of marking time. Our modern calendar uses numeric values to measure periods, and numbers as markers for identifying the milestones and events that we celebrate. But events are merely collections of moments in time, and even the best events contain moments unworthy of celebration. We would leave such moments behind to be buried by the passing of time, if only we could. If only the number marking that date would not return every year, as a cursed reminder.

The relentless rattle of gunfire finally began to weaken, reduced to isolated pops that joined the chorus of moans from injured survivors. The streets of Puebla lay covered in blood; smoke and ash filled its air. But the end to the battle was at hand. Every soldier could sense it. Including Hector, who seized the opportunity and positioned himself between his dying brother and the injured, defenseless soldier who had shot him just moments ago. Now, the attacker begged for mercy.

Hector wasn't interested in mercy. These foreigners invaded his homeland. This one in particular had just injured his brother, maybe fatally. Why should he show mercy?

The foreigner continued his plea. "Listen... do you hear it?" he said. "The battle is ending. You have won. If you kill me now, you will be nothing but a murderer."

"I will be a hero, just like my comrades and my brother here, who fought along my side to defend our home and family from dogs like you," replied Hector defiantly.

"Spare my life. Get help for your brother before he dies."

"Maybe. Or maybe I kill you first?" Hector's words hid the fact that he was torn. He wanted to pull his brother to safety. But he loathed the thought of his prisoner's escape.

"Don't be a fool. You can still save him."

"Silence," said Hector, unsure of his next move.

The foreigner changed his tactic. "Your people have fought bravely, this is true. They will undoubtedly celebrate this day for many years to come. But if you kill me... this day will mean nothing but eternal misery for you and your brother. I curse you... if you pull that trigger, may you forever be damned. On this day each year, while your children and your children's children celebrate, may you know nothing of peace. May you only know pain and suff..."

A single shot from Hector's gun ended the conversation.

"Dammit, Jesse, my glass is empty! Get me another drink! And get my friend here one, too. He'll appreciate it once he wakes up!" Scott pushed his empty rocks glass to the edge of the bar, hoping the fear of glass shattering across the scuffed wooden floor would bring Jesse running. Scott glared at Jesse as he chose to serve an attractive female seated across the bar.

Slapping the bar top, he clamored, "Methinks my good man Jesse here is ignoring me on purpose. Just because I'm a regular, he thinks I don't mind waiting. Well, I do." With the buzz from his last drink fading too quickly for his liking, Scott turned the heat up on his request.

"Hey, Jesse! You ain't gonna get laid. No pussy for you. She just wants you because you're serving her under-age ass drinks. Yeah, you heard me, she's underage. LCB is gonna bust you man. No pussy is worth that."

Scott snatched the rocks glass and crunched the last specks of the tequila-infused ice. Unable to tear Jesse away, he reluctantly sat back and watched the show.

"Well, it *might* be worth it. She's got nice tits. I bet they're real too." He continued his monologue to no one in particular. "What do you think? Real or Memorex? Ha! You remember that audio cassette commercial, don't you? Ah, the fucking 80's. Or was it the 70's? Who cares, it was a great commercial."

Stealing his bloodshot eyes away from the underage breasts was a sizzling plate of fajitas, as it made its grand entrance from the kitchen to the table behind him.

"Jesus, those look good. I could eat, but it would just get in the way of my buzz. Why eat when you can get fucked up? Speaking of fucked up: hey, Jesse, do I have to get my own drink? I'm dehydrating over here!"

At the new home of the sizzling fajita plate, a small group of men cleared the table of empty Corona bottles to make room for the incoming meal. As the group began assembling their dinner, one of them raised a shot glass.

"Happy Cinco de Mayo!"

"Bah," said another seated at the table, drunk and slurring each word. "You don't even know what you're drinking to."

Meanwhile, Scott continued his tirade at the front bar to anyone within earshot.

"Speaking of little pricks, I just heard my ex-wife split up with the bastard she left me for because she couldn't live with the size of his dick. There's no pleasing that woman, no matter what size your schlong. She said I drank too much. Well guess what? I drank less before I met her, so what does that say? I still can't believe she left me when my health started going down the shitter. For better or for worse, my cock-sucking ass. She's one stone cold bitch."

Cringing at the song blaring from the jukebox, Scott rose from his perch.

"How many times do I have to hear 'Tequila' tonight? That's the fourth time since I sat my fat ass down. There's gotta be something else on that box. Hey, buddy, if Jesse comes around, get me a margarita, a pink fruity one." The imagery brought him to laughter, momentarily distracting him from his tirade.

"Nah, just fucking with ya. Get me a double shot of bourbon. I need to mix things up a little tonight. Get yourself whatever you like, it's on me. I gotta slip a dollar in that little slut's hungry slot so she'll sing to me. Don't look at me like that; she likes it when I talk dirty."

As Scott rambled, his bar mate remained face-down, preferring the comfort of the sticky wood bar to the company of Scott and his endless yammering.

Back at the rear table, the drunken man at the fajita table continued his own banter. "Do you even know why this day is celebrated? Do you know about the battle of Puebla?"

A series of blank stares answered his question.

The jukebox roared a final "Tequila," and began the next song in the queue. Scott didn't recognize it. Stumbling to the touch screen on the wall, he watched a few seconds of a perplexing music video and was overwhelmed at the seemingly endless song selection. After a few moments of intense study, he decided it was best to spend his money at the bar instead of making a musical faux pas at the jukebox.

Strolling back to the more familiar territory, he was hoping to find a fresh glass full of booze waiting for him. Instead, he found his barstool occupied by an oversized woman stuffed into sequined pink spandex. He watched for a moment as she busied herself with a cell phone, stopping long enough to take a sip of a frozen daiquiri. He scooted to the other side of his friend, and then glared again at the woman.

"Who the fuck does she think she is? How the hell did this bitch rate to get a drink? And what in God's name is her ass eating? I think it attacked the Easter Bunny. Man, I'd punch her in the face... if I didn't think her ass would eat me."

As Scott ranted on, Jesse appeared and set a heaping plate of nachos in front of the woman before quickly floating back towards the other end of the bar. Incredulous, Scott yipped, "Son of a bitch, nachos?"

Back at the table, the drunken man began his slurred history lesson.

"Cinco de Mayo, my ass. Here's what happened... once upon a time, the French invaded the Mexican state of Puebla with a massive army. They were the best army in the world. They could have defeated anyone... even America."

Almost on cue, another group near the front bar began chanting "U-S-A... U-S-A" as a man with a Mexican flag tattoo on his bicep was engaged in a heated arm wrestling match with another sporting an American flag. It was enough of a spectacle to distract the group from the remnants of their fajitas.

Undeterred, the drunken man among them continued.

"Anyone. They could have conquered the world. But these Mexicans... they got lucky. A small group—half the size of the French troops—defeated them. The date was May 5, 1862. May 5th... or 'Cinco de Mayo', as they say south of the border," the man said sarcastically. He raised his hands in the air feigning victory.

"The Day of the Battle of Puebla. That, gentlemen, is why we drink today. Because of a bunch of lucky Mexicans."

At the bar, Scott's anger began to grow.

"I can't get so much as a glass of 'fuck you' and this bitch gets nachos?" he said, pounding his hand on the bar. "I bet if I had a set of tits...or a voracious pink ass he'd wait on me. Although, pink's not my best color. What do you think?" He slapped his neighbor on the back. The man didn't rouse.

"Come on man, it's Cinco De Mayo. Time to wake the fuck up." Attempting to nudge his neighbor's shoulder, the man slid from his perch and fell prostrate onto the grimy bar floor, right in front of the ongoing arm wrestling battle.

"Awww... shit. Come on, man. Don't fucking do this. Get up."

Scott began to panic.

"Somebody help him! Jesus people, why the hell are you just sitting there?" He shrieked in the woman's face. "A man is on the ground and all you can do is eat nachos? You selfish fucking bitch. Somebody help me! Jesse! Jesse, you worthless fuck, call 911."

Within seconds, paramedics pushed through the front doors of the bar. Two men carrying a stretcher and a large medic bag knelt beside the man lying at Scott's feet.

Despite the fact that his audience had long since left him to watch the scene at the front of the bar, the drunken man back at the fajita table continued on about the history of this day.

"Cinco de Mayo. May 5, 1862. The Day of the Battle of Puebla. I remember it. I remember it like it was yesterday," he said, to no one there.

Giving the medics room to work, Scott stepped back and into the table behind him, where the combatants surprisingly continued their match, now in front of a large crowd of spectators. In anger, he lashed out.

"How can you be so callous? What does it take for you people to give a fuck around here?"

After working feverishly for several minutes, the paramedics loaded the body of the fallen man onto the stretcher. Just before covering his face, Scott was able to finally catch a glimpse of his languid drinking buddy.

He immediately recognized the face. It had been exactly one year since he had last seen it. A lot had changed in the past year. But one thing hadn't changed. It has never changed, each time. That face. His brother's face.

"If only you had called for us earlier... even a few minutes... maybe we could have saved him," said one of the paramedics.

Scott turned to see the drunken man from the fajita table, now standing at his side.

"Hello Hector. Or Scott, or whatever you're calling yourself this year. Happy 5th of May, you lucky Mexican murderer."

Scott's head hung low as he began to process the scene. As always, the facts and the memories suddenly came rushing back to him, like a gust of ash-filled wind from that old battlefield in Puebla. As they did he cupped his face in his hands, desperately attempting to avoid the returning horror.

"I see you let your brother die again," said the drunken man, now fully clothed in his bloody French militia uniform. He slapped his old adversary on the shoulder.

"Same old Hector. Happy anniversary, you bastard. See you next year."

These Six Walls

Recurring numbers can be found throughout the natural world. Most starfish have five appendages, and if one is lost it will even regenerate to maintain that number. Snowflakes offer us six-fold symmetrical designs, every time. Are such manifestations random designs, or is there is something more to the numerical symmetry and balance of nature? What is the true essence of the relationship between nature and its numeric values?

"Secretary General, these are dire times," croaked U.S. President Marie Carosella. She had addressed the United Nations many times in recent months, but her words today were much more urgent. Today's meeting was an emergency session, and the mood of the entire assembly was somber. She did her best to maintain a calm confidence as she continued.

"With the fortitude and unprecedented cooperation of each of your governments, we collectively have succeeded in providing the people of the world with sustainable resources. We have conquered global hunger, rendering all fallow land viable for food production. We have generated the technology to attain safe, clean drinking water from salt and brackish water across the globe. We have enforced sufficient clean air legislation to stabilize the world's atmosphere and temperature by reversing the actions of companies and corporations that ignored all indicators of global warming.

"These efforts have made the human race stronger than at any other time in our history. In addition, we have made advances that have transformed the medical community. We no longer worry about ancient maladies such as cancer, childhood diseases, or deadly infections that were once a death sentence. The United States is proud to stand with you and declare that, together, we have transformed the world."

Thunderous applause filled the room. For at least a few moments, those gathered were able to feel good again. But, as President Carosella's speech continued, her audience was quickly returned to its darker focus.

"As you know, this transformation has not come without a price. We are unable to celebrate these successes that have taken decades to fulfill, because we are now faced with a challenge that dwarfs all those of our past. Our greatest success as a species now has led us to the precipice of what could potentially become our greatest failure. Overpopulation and overcrowding now threatens our very existence." The hall exploded in mini-discussions as clusters of UN members aired their personal concerns. Unable to regain control of the audience, President Carosella waved in gratitude to those eyes still fixed on her, and conceded the floor.

The Secretary General stood up to quell the rumblings and address the General Assembly. He ran his hand through his thick silver head of hair and spoke with all the confidence of a fit and active 78-year-old man in his prime. The boisterous gathering settled long enough to hear his words.

"We all share President Carosella's deep concern for the wellbeing of our member nations and the world at large. Conditions are now taxing the very terra that we worked so hard to salvage, rebuild, and support. The land cannot support man and his sustenance. It is being crushed under the weight of all we've managed to accomplish.

"Never before has the world needed the efforts of the United Nations as much as it now does. I urge you to keep that in mind as we proceed here. The Board of Habitation and Communal Development has devised..."

The Secretary General paused, struggling to finish his words. His demeanor was that of a frightened child standing at the edge of the ocean, afraid to even touch a toe into the water. With a gulp, he proceeded.

"Well, they have devised a plan. If successful, this plan will have a dramatic impact on the explosion of population that now presents the biggest threat to humankind ever faced. You may find the ideas you are about to hear to be highly controversial. But I beg you, for the sake of our very existence, hear them out."

With that, the Secretary General called upon Madame Burns of Ireland, Chair of the Board of Habitation and Communal Development, to address the assembly.

"The housing plan mandate is quite simple," she began, being careful to deemphasize the word 'mandate.' "We propose the development of worldwide housing, to be constructed vertically. Massive group complexes comprised solely of individual hexagonal units."

A murmur began to make its way across the assembly floor. The Secretary General stood and waved his hands down, silently asking those in attendance to remain quiet.

"These complexes will be high rises, which we have dubbed 'Hive Rises.' She nodded to an assistant, who generated a rotating hologram.

"Our engineers have studied more designs than I can possibly share with you. These men and women represent the brightest minds in engineering and structural design. And they are unanimous in their beliefs about the potential of this one. Six-sided structures, or 'cells', if you will. Each adjacent to others on all six sides. This honeycomb design provides such strength structurally that we will be able to build structures taller than any the planet has ever seen. The design also makes absolute maximum use of space, ensuring the largest number of residents can reside comfortably in the smallest footprint of land. This design also enables the provision of personal space. Each cell will have the exact same dimensions, designed for efficient use by one—and only one—person. With regard to families, each cell will connect to a family member's cell, ensuring domestic functionality. Some of your countries have already been fortuitous enough to experience beta models of Hive Rises during the testing period. The valuable lessons we have learned there have led us to finalize our designs. We can now declare with certainty that this is the most valuable and viable housing option to ensure our existence—without compromising our resources."

Again, pockets of conversations broke out across the assembly. Quietly at first, then growing into near chaos.

"This is madness," declared the ambassador from the U.K., to no one in particular. "They'll have us living in bloody beehives."

"The people will revolt," proclaimed an Ecuadorian assistant to her ambassador. "We will have uprisings around the world. We cannot simply mandate public housing!"

It took nearly twenty minutes for the Secretary General to regain order in the hall. Once he did, he scanned the room with the look of a father about to share bad news with his children.

"Ladies and gentlemen, the debate is useless. We all knew coming into this session that drastic measures are required. It breaks my heart to even consider such radical plans, but there is no other way. We must enforce mandated housing in these efficient cells, or we are doomed as a species. I implore you to vote 'yes' to this plan.

"Your governments will receive information necessary to begin the Hive Rise constructions as soon as possible. Our agenda is aggressive. Groundbreaking would begin in North America, just as soon as our vote is confirmed. Within the next fifty years, every country on the planet would be converted. By the end of 2578, all land not suitable for food production will be sourced for housing."

He rubbed his tired eyes for a moment, and then returned them to the worried crowd.

"Now, I suggest we cease the debate and begin our vote. Our fate is before us."

The three-day emergency session ended much more quietly than it began. A desperate U.N. Assembly unanimously passed the plan. As soon as the results were known, members scurried home to their nations. There was much work to do.

"And now, the news at the top of the hour... police were called to yet another violent incident, this one at one of the Sussex County West End Colonies. Witnesses report that the violence began with two men who were found to be loitering outside the block of cells. A small group of cell citizens allegedly became alarmed as the victims strayed into the cell block and became boisterous. As our own Jenny Rodriguez reports, three residents armed with baseball bats are reported to have confronted the trespassers. Witnesses say it was then that the fight broke out. Jenny is live at the scene. Jenny, what more can you tell us at this hour?"

Edward flipped off the holovision and sighed. He lifted himself from his chair and shuffled his way to the door of the adjoining cell. As he swung the door open, he was met by a cold glance from his wife, who seemed perturbed by her husband's intrusion.

"What now? You know I'm watching my stories."

Edward pointed to the holovision image that held her attention. "I just saw there was another attack, this time in Colony 42, not that far from here. This is the fifth attack in the area's colonies this month," he said, hoping his wife would understand the urgency. She didn't.

"Why do you watch the news? It just riles you up. Do you know how many colonies there are? And you're worried about five isolated incidents,"

Edward interrupted her, "Yes, I know how many colonies there are. I helped build them, remember? And there have been five incidents in our area. The same stuff is happening elsewhere, Marcia. You'd know this if you'd watch something with some substance to it."

Marcia continued as if she didn't hear him. "We haven't had one problem in our colony, not one. So stop being such an alarmist. Ed, you're not a scientist anymore. You're a retired 118-year-old man who can't shut his damn mind off, so he sits and worries about crap that he doesn't need to worry about. Get a hobby, preferably one that doesn't include me."

Edward shrugged off Marcia's words and shuffled back to his own cell. He returned to his recliner and began speaking, mostly to himself but knowing Marcia would hear.

"I don't understand... it's been nearly fifty years since the last of the revolts. Just when it seemed the world had come to accept it all, now we have this. I remember all those hours...

the countless debates in those meetings. We knew there'd be trouble in implementing this. But not like this. Once the revolts had been suppressed, we figured people would learn to be happy. No more struggling to carve out a spot. Everyone has their own space. It's theirs."

Edward paused to look out his solitary window. As an original member of the U.N. Board of Habitation and Communal Development who helped plan and implement the cells, he was awarded one with an outside view, overlooking a small patch of land used for recreation by the residents. He often peered out this window and reflected on the events of the past half-century.

"Why are they behaving like this?" he continued. "Everyone has a cell just like everyone else. Exactly the same. Why are people behaving so angrily? Why are they so protective?"

It was then that the idea first occurred to him.

"No. It can't be..."

Anxiously, he opened his trusty journal and began to scribble notes and calculations.

"There's no scientific reason for it. None whatsoever. Still, I must consider it. I need to learn more."

The community literary cells, which contained public network access and crystal micro data of published research, were only a few blocks away. An easy walk that he enjoyed taking on a regular basis.

"I'll be back in a bit, dear," he shouted to his wife in her adjacent cell. With that, he hurried out the exit walks and made his way outside. Having led the design of this community, he knew it by memory. He decided to take a shortcut around the back of block 417.

It was there that he was attacked. It was over quickly.

"Awww... Mom. I don't wanna help with the babies today. It's boring down there. Why can't I hang out with you in your cell?" Kapryce whined, defiantly crossing her arms and huffing.

"You don't have to do anything, so why should I?" she added.

"We all have a job to do in this world; helping Ms. Regula and Ms. Hobbs with the babies is yours."

"I know, Mom. You tell me this every day. I know the babies are special," she said sarcastically. "It's just not fair. I bet things would be different if Dad were here."

Kapryce's mother Misti raised her voice from her own cell. She turned to Kapryce and said "There is no need to speak of your father. He feels the same way. Besides he is here. Just not... here."

Kapryce's mom knew what this defiance was about. At ten years old, Kapryce was just old enough to remember. It had only been seven years since their colony, like most others around the world, had voted to relocate male residents to lower floors of their Hive Rise, where they could more easily make their way in and out to better handle their colony chores. Male residents were now asked to work collectively to retrieve food and supplies to support the colony; this required frequent trips away from the Hive Rises. Those not tasked with the frequent trips out were assigned to the ground floor warehouses, stocking supplies as they arrived. Others were tasked with security patrol around the main entrances. All of these duties required significant time on the lower levels. So males were assigned cells away from their families, who dwelled on the higher floors. The relocation was hard on families, and especially on children like Kapryce. But it was the most efficient use of space assignments.

While Misti accepted that Kapryce's behavior was in part due to the adjustment of a split home, she also knew that what her daughter really wanted to do today was stay in her cell. She had become a hermit of sorts. She rarely wanted to leave her cell and play with the other children in the colony. Misti had grown concerned about it, to the point of talking about this with her teachers at the colony school. They assured her that other parents had reported similar behavior from their children and that, while it was being investigated by school officials, they currently saw no reason for alarm.

Misti made her way into Kapryce's cell and found her in the usual spot; sitting on her suspended cot. "These Six Walls," the latest hit from some group whose name she could not even pronounce, blared loudly from the ceiling-mounted audio player.

"What are you doing, dear?" asked Misti, pinching her fingers toward the ceiling to lower the volume.

"Reading the old book again."

"Again? I thought I asked you to toss that thing out. There is simply no room for extras like that. We may even get in trouble if the Colony Patrol finds it. You know the rules... we must maintain efficient use of..."

"I know, I know..." interrupted Kapryce. "We must maintain efficient use of space. But I like it, Momma. Did Great-great-grandpa really write all of the stories in here?"

Misti scooted next to Kapryce on the cot. These conversations were always difficult. It had been well over 200 years since the "lifestyle conversion", as it was now commonly referred. Kapryce's great-great grandfather Edward had led the way, serving as lead engineer on the U.N. HCD Board. It was his design that most credited for saving humankind. But like many children of this era, Kapryce struggled to understand the realities of the past.

"They're not really stories, but I can see why you like them. He was a smart man, one of the most brilliant men of his time. He wrote many things."

"I like the last story best."

"He was old and sick by then, dear. The poor man could no longer think clearly. He even wandered off and got too close to another colony. That old journal was found near his body, and it is all we have left of him now. But I'm afraid most of his last entries are the nonsensical ramblings of a sick and delusional old man. Don't remember him by his last days. Remember all the good that he did. Some people say he saved the world. He helped create our efficient housing; 'these six walls', as your noisy friends say." Misti smiled and pointed toward the ceiling speaker.

"You should be proud to be his great-great-granddaughter."

"Does everyone have great-great-granddaughters?"

"No dear. Some people are not born to have children. We all have a job to do in this world."

"Stay away from our colony! It's not our problem that yours failed. Ask the government for a rebuild," yelled one vocal woman from her third floor cell window.

A middle-aged woman in her nineties pushed towards the swarm of people waiting to storm the colony. Like others of her kind, she rarely came outside. Some eighty years ago, she was among the first to be diagnosed with "Extrocel Phobia," a tendency to avoid leaving the Hive Rise unless absolutely necessary. She recalled how much she hated when her mother would make it a necessity, all to help take care of younger ones. Now, she had a new reason to step outside. This confrontation with the neighboring colony had the potential of attack, and she was prepared to defend her home.

"You should have taken better care of yourselves. I've been watching. You refused to tend to your garden and watched it rot. You let your men's numbers grow out of control and now they have eaten you out of your fall and winter food supply. Your fertile women are becoming whores, engaging in sex with anyone, while your daughters become slovenly, lazy and unwilling to pride themselves with taking care of their community home. You've let your cells crumble and fall into disrepair, and you expect us to come to your aid? Well, we cannot and will not!"

A band of inhabitants from the intact colony cheered and raised their hands in solidarity. The agitation from the crowd grew fiercer with each word.

The spokesperson for the fallen colony pushed through the tightly packed crowd and came face to face with her rival. She was a little younger than the other woman, but just as defiant. She smirked at her older accuser, showing off her chipped and yellowed teeth.

"We don't want your aid, do we?" The mob itching behind her screamed, "No!" as if they all practiced their succinct reply.

"Then what do you want?" the older woman said, unprepared for the answer.

Still smirking, the woman reached into her back pants pocket and with one swift blow she gutted her rival with a blade. As her body slumped into the thick grass, the trespasser's smirk became a hideous smile.

"We want your colony."

It was late in the day. Soon, night would fall. Most members of the Area 42 colonies were trying to make their way back to their hives before nightfall. The streets connecting each area were a bustle of activity. Huge masses of people made their way home, carrying baskets of food for the young. The congestion made it nearly impossible to take more than a few steps without making contact with others, sometimes knocking baskets of food over or causing human pileups resembling the interstate multicar accidents of some 900 years ago. But the violence such events would have caused then was nowhere to be seen now. People calmly, purposefully picked their belongings up and carried on. There were no conversations, no apologies for the contact. Only blank stares. And an undeterred determination to get the food home to the young before nightfall. This was the only purpose.

Just outside of block 2133, a young man stared at an artifact from an ancient time. The markings inside were hard to interpret. Almost no one had any knowledge of the ancient English language anymore, especially in print. But the man treasured this artifact, a family heirloom passed down over hundreds of generations. He practiced daily, deciphering the words.

"Must... consider..."

He struggled over each word.

"Must... consider... design. Flaw. Six... sided cell." He paused, frustrated and unsure if he was pronouncing the words properly—and even less sure of their meaning.

"Six sided cell. Ho-ney...comb. Could...make...people..."

The light was fading. He knew he had to be inside now.

"Could... make... people... behave..."

Rushing the pace only further contributed to his frustration. He knew what darkness meant. But he was so close to finishing now. He pushed on to complete the final sentence.

"Could... make... people... behave..."

Confused, he finished the final words.

"...like bees."

The words had no meaning to him. It was just as well, they had many times in the distant past been labeled as the nonsensical ramblings of a sick and delusional old man. Many hundreds of years ago, the author himself had confirmed that there was no scientific reason to believe them.

There was no choice now. The reader had to stop for the evening. He reburied the artifact in the usual spot. Tomorrow would be another day. He methodically made his way into the hive, past his cell and toward Her chamber. Just as every other night, he waited in line for his turn to enter the large cell and bow before his queen.

As he entered the chamber, she summoned the young man to her. Instinctively he knew what this meant. There, without word, they had intercourse. His mission complete, he left her and exited the chamber.

A small group of men approached him upon his exit. He also knew what this meant. He bowed his head, satisfied in the thought that he had efficiently fulfilled his purpose. The men struck quickly, just as attackers had against his forefather so many years before. The body was carried off by two others.

The remaining residents entered their cells for rest. They would need it. The queen would give birth soon. There would be a need to construct more cells. And gather more food.

Seven Colors

To the untrained eye, a rainbow is a spectacle of nature and the stuff of wonder and fantasy. To those trained in science, rainbows are a product of the properties of light and its spectrum of seven distinct colors. As so it is with numbers; they offer mystery to some of us and explanation to others. But maybe every once in a while these two paradigms can learn something from each other.

"I'm gonna kill you, you errant little bastard!"

Michael lobbed horseshoes at Biggleton's head in a fit of sheer rage. He was far from athletic, but by the luck of the Irish one of the wayward horseshoes nicked his target in the shin, toppling him over. Michael sprung on top of his adversary and pinned him to the cold laboratory floor.

"I only gave you what you wished for, laddie," Biggleton proclaimed, amidst moans and yelps of pain. "So please let me up from this foul parquet. I believe there's iron up my arse from those damned horseshoes." His pleas did little to loosen the grip the scientist had on him.

"Just look at yourself," he continued. "This isn't you, Mikey. You're not a killer. You're a man of science. Remember, Mikey, you brought *me* into *your* life, and it has been nothing short of magical."

Michael hated that Biggleton was right. But even more than that, he hated the 'errant little bastard.'

It was a Sunday, and Michael had everything planned to specifications. Only on this day could the classical planetary spheres could be seen with the naked eye from his laboratory window. This seemed the perfect day to launch his prodigious experiment. The prism pyramid had taken years to be erected and now, finally, it was ready to be tested.

A young physicist already accomplished in the field of optics, Michael devoted his career to studying the properties of light. For years, the primary focus of his research was the spectrum of light: the seven primary colors that combine to form light as is typically seen by the rest of us. Many people enjoy rainbows. But where most individuals view a naturally-occurring spectacle of nature, Michael perceived seven primary light phases refracted and reflected onto water vapors in the sky.

Although his research focused on separating and recombining the seven colors of light, his data hinged on the arcane question of why light behaves as it does. If he were able to penetrate that mysterious membrane, his work would become groundbreaking and change the world's understanding of light theory. Along the way, it would also win him accolades from the research community, something Michael secretly craved since the days of his graduate dissertation.

So on that particular Sunday, Michael was understandably anxious. With the eagerness of a child on Christmas morning, he scurried about the laboratory making his final preparations. With everything in place, he turned off the lights, and calibrated the prism. He even selected the eclectic music of "World Beats" from his digital radio station to create a little mood for his light show.

At first, the prism simply glowed white. Within seconds, however, it radiated a fantastic beam of fractured light from the tip of the structure to the high laboratory ceiling. All seven colors of the spectrum, perfectly dispersed. Step One of his experiment was already a success. Michael smiled at the dazzling rainbow and eagerly studied the readings from his computer. His fingers furiously assaulted the keys, capturing detailed notes. The apparatus he spent years developing was fully functional, and it was beautiful. Michael was so proud and confident he could almost taste the words from his Nobel acceptance speech that would sate his mentors and leave his peers hungry for more.

But his indulgence was short lived. Twenty-two minutes into his experiment, the spectral light emitting from the top of the pyramid turned the color of mud. The machine screamed, as if it were alive and being torn apart from the inside. Obsessively punching the escape key, Michael hissed, "No, no, no! This shouldn't be happening."

A soulful melody from Ireland emanated from the computer's speakers, which made the ugly brown light ripple and seize with fervor. Fearing the pyramid's total destruction, Michael ran to cut the power from the source. But his urgency was for naught. The sounds from the prism were debilitating. Involuntarily, Michael snapped his eyes shut and cupped his ears. The ensuing blast caused him to ricochet off the table and trip halfway across the room, spilling the contents of his lab coat pockets all over the floor.

Crawling on his belly, Michael made his way to the pyramid. He snatched the plug from the wall and lay like a beached whale on the lab floor. There he remained, overcome by grief and unable to do more than stare at the ceiling.

His disappointment was quickly curtailed by a high pitched whistle. At first Michael assumed the music was coming from his radio. But this was no "World Beats" offering.

"This is a rather interesting find," exclaimed a voice. Michael quickly scanned the room but saw nothing. Suddenly, from his spot on the floor, he saw a pair of impeccable shoes approach him. He lifted his head and sat in shock at the short distance his eyes needed to travel. There, no more than two and a half feet from the floor, stood a man. Only in miniature.

The wee man was sporting green knickers and a ratty gray shirt. He was holding a Sacajawea dollar coin that had rolled from Michael's lab coat pocket. The little man jumped from the pyramid beside Michael and inspected his new find.

"Well, it ain't gold, but methinks it'll do."

Mesmerized by the startling grand entrance of the wee man from the bowels of the pyramid, Michael could only stare.

"Cat got your tongue, laddie?" he chortled. "It's been a long time since one of your kin caught hold of one of our kith. How'd you do it?"

Michael rubbed his eyes, mumbling unintelligibly. Pocketing the coin, the tiny man sighed.

"Aye, an eejit are we? Well eejit, me name is Biggleton. So now that you've made my acquaintance, pray tell how the feck you brought me here."

Michael felt the words slowly drip from his tongue. He seemed to question them even as they left his own mouth.

"The pyramid. The prism. The light. Somehow, I guess... I mean... the seven colors... the rainbow... and..."

As Michael struggled for an explanation, he reached for his twisted glasses which had skated across the floor. He set them on the bridge of his nose, as if seeing more clearly would somehow help him to see *this* more clearly.

"Are you a... leprechaun? But... leprechauns aren't real."

Biggleton snorted and snatched a lit pipe from the pocket of his britches. He was oblivious to any further explanation Michael was struggling to provide.

"Damned rainbows, bent on causing trouble to me kith. Next, you'll be clamoring you aren't trying to nick me gold."

Michael opened his mouth to speak, but was quickly spat upon from the leprechaun's oncoming fit.

"Bollocks! Mankind wants nothing more than to exploit us for our spoils. I was content lounging by the Meloys' wood pile getting pissed by me self and I end up... I end up... where did you conjure me to, boyo?"

"You're in a laboratory. I'm a scientist. I was experimenting with light. I don't understand how this happened." Stretching his fingers to touch the manifestation in front of him, Michael's hand was violently smacked with Biggleton's smoldering pipe.

"Keep your hands to yourself, ya poof. There may be no female leprechauns, but I'm no knob gobbler."

Michael perched himself on a rolling stool and backed away from the affronted imp.

"I wasn't trying... I just can't believe you're real. I've read about you in fairy tales, but I never believed the stories to be true."

"You can't believe everything you read, boyo. For example, we don't come out on St. Patty's Day and drink beer and dance jigs. Lies, I tell ya. We do it all the time, not just St. Patrick's Day. Oh and as for St. Patrick, he was a pansy-arsed steamer. He was bleeding afraid of snakes... unless they were in some fella's cackers."

Not listening to a word out of Biggleton's lips, Michael sputtered, "If you're real, then you are a genuine scientific find. This could be... huge! Bigger than my plans to crack the mysteries of light. I can prove the existence of a being thought to be from mythos!"

Suddenly, Michael's eyes opened wide. As his thoughts raced from disbelief to scientific superstardom, yet another thought crossed his now scattered mind.

"Do you really have a pot of gold?"

A yellow flame exploded in Biggleton's green eyes. "So ya *are* after me gold!"

Michael rolled his stool into the corner, far away from the imp's wrath. "No! I'm not after your gold. I just want to know if it's true what they say about leprechauns and pots of gold. Because if it is, we need to get you somewhere safe. People will try and exploit you for their own gains. But you're too important to the scientific community to let that happen. Against my better judgment, you're going to have to come home with me."

Biggleton hopped up on a lab table littered with paper data and began dancing to a song from the computer speakers.

"Well, since you caught me fair and square... and I can't seem to disappear from your presence... your place it is. But can we wait for this melody to finish?"

Michael's house looked exactly like the laboratory; white, sterile and devoid of personal touches. Everything was carefully arranged and nothing was out of place. Biggleton bounded through the opened door and leapt onto the couch.

Kicking off his well-hewed shoes, he propped his feet on the immaculate coffee table.

"You got a nice place here, Mikey boy. Could you fetch me an ale? Oh, and where exactly do you stash your porn?"

"Look here... Biggleton. This is just temporary until I figure out what to do with you. I need time to think."

Michael made his way to the kitchen, and returned with a beer from the refrigerator. The tiny visitor sucked the offering down in one impressive swallow.

"Ah. Mam's milk, if I were to have a mam. Speaking of females, where is yours?" With that, Biggleton hurled the empty glass bottle over his shoulder.

"Jesus." Michael whimpered, scurrying to grab the broom and clean up the shards.

"Watch your gob, boyo. My ears are virgin to cussing in that manner. Hummm, no female, eh?" Biggleton lifted the cushions from the sofa.

"So, you keep your pornography where?"

"I don't keep any pornography, all right? I'm a scientist, and a busy one at that. I'm this close to winning a Nobel Prize. As corny as it sounds, science is my lady."

"Science is your lady? Well... are you sure you aren't a poof? Since you're up, laddie, can you get me another ale? Ah, never mind, I'll get it me self."

Biggleton leapt from his perch on the couch and hopped to the refrigerator for a beer. Inside, he found a few other selections that piqued his interest. He settled on an unopened package of shredded jalapeno cheese.

"Ooh, what is this?"

He grabbed fistfuls of the cheese and gobbled it down. Within seconds the floor in front of the refrigerator was littered with bits of cheese. Gathering up the last of the glass with a wet rag, Michael watched in horror as his new house guest poured the cheesy goodness into his mouth, most of the contents missing its target.

"What are you doing? We use a bowl when we eat. Christ, you're making a mess!"

"Watch your gob! Ah shite! What kind of devil cheese is this? It's delicious but it's burning me face off. I can't seem to stop eating it. Shite, I need more beer to quell the beastly fire!"

As if ridding a fly, he flicked off the bottle cap and hastily chugged a beer. Followed by another and yet another. Within minutes he had drained the lone six-pack in the refrigerator, topping off his performance with a deafening and offensive belch.

"Aye, boyo, that was some cheese. Got any more?"

Before Michael could answer, a guttural growl echoed from the imp's belly, stealing both their attention.

"Devil cheese! The bastard is trying to make his way out. Where's your dirty woodpile, boyo?"

A confused Michael stammered, "There is no dirty woodpile."

Scott unbuckled his pants and assumed a squatting position. Horrified, Michael was frozen as he watched.

"Well, this evil cunt isn't going to wait until you get one. God have mercy on my soul! Turn your head, boyo. Have some manners."

Before the imp could taint his kitchen any further, Michael plucked Biggleton from the squatting position and awkwardly carried him to the bathroom. The leprechaun was helpless, dangling, cursing and clutching himself the whole way. Michael plopped him on the commode and slammed the door behind him. Rattled by the ungodly sounds and the nose-hair curling stench that poured from the bathroom, he ran his hands through his thinning hair and groaned.

"Maybe this was a big mistake."

Hours had passed since the jalapeno cheese disaster, and, surprisingly, Michael found himself hungry. Biggleton, who had left the refrigerator empty, was now napping beneath the dining room table. Since his visitor was asleep, Michael decided to zip down the street to the convenience store for something to eat.

His hand hadn't even turned the doorknob to make his exit when Biggleton punched him in the meat of his thigh.

"Where ya off to, laddie? Pulling out like a Catholic is one of my old tricks."

Michael sighed. "I'm going to grab something quick for dinner. Is there anything in particular that your people like to eat? Besides cheese?"

Biggleton rubbed his calloused little hands together. "I do believe you're out of ale. We can't have that. You know, since your last selection was dreadful, perhaps I'll come along and find a right manly draught, preferably one we can chew."

Michael leaned against the door, "I don't think it's a good idea to be out in public."

The leprechaun grabbed hold of Michael's pant leg, climbed up his lanky frame and poked a finger in his nose.

"Dammit ya bleeding cunt, you're taking me with you! But before we go, change your shirt and comb your hair. No lass is gonna want to shag ya looking like a langer."

The convenience store was bustling with customers purchasing their vices of cigarettes, coffee and soda. The lingering scent of cold cuts, blackened pizza and desiccated wieners from the self-serve melded together. Michael was relieved that most of the patrons couldn't be bothered to give the tiny man a second nod between grabbing a newspaper and lecturing their gluttonous children on the merits of not whining when they heard the word "no."

The ample selection of brews in the coolers made Biggleton's yellow eyes bulge and his parched lips quiver. Reaching into the cooler for a favored stout, he was interrupted by a drunk male eyeing up the same brand as the imp.

"Yo, bro. Looks like we both have the same taste in beer."

The drunk rocked back and forth as he bent down to get a better view of his brother-in-beer. He finally held steady long enough to take the sight in.

"This is sick, bro, has anyone told you that you that you look just like that dude from the cereal box? So where's your pot of gold?"

Flames burst from Biggleton's yellow eyes and hop-scented venom spewed from his lips. "Are ye startin', Dickbrain? Fair Dig!"

And with that, the leprechaun leapt at the drunk's face, latching onto his nose with his teeth. The drunk flopped on his back and squealed as Biggleton pummeled his head with his petite but robust fists.

"I'm gonna wind your neck in, ya bastard!" The uproar caused a small crowd to muster, enflaming the one-sided melee with the chant, "Go, dwarf, go! Go, dwarf, go!" Dropping his partially mustard-topped hot dog, Michael raced towards the clamor. The leprechaun had the drunk pinned to the floor and was beating him with a loaf of bread someone had donated to the battle for added entertainment. Bloody spittle sprayed from the drunk's broken lips as he screamed for help.

"Get him off me! He's fucking crazy. Somebody help me!"

After a few awkward minutes of yanking the angry imp from his victim, Michael finally wrenched him free. He heaved Biggleton over his shoulder and shoved his way through the disappointed crowd and out of the store, but not without a barrage of Irish curses spewing from the enraged leprechaun.

"May your anus be knotted! I hope your obituary is written in the foulest weasel piss! May the cat eat you and the devil eat the cat! If me brothers were here with me, you'd be eating hospital food. That's right, ya manky git, hospital food!"

Bursting through his apartment door, Michael tossed the irate leprechaun on his couch.

"What the hell was that?" he yelled. "Drawing attention to yourself before the world is ready to accept what you are will get you hurt, or maybe even killed!"

"That arse was talking shite. He's lucky to still be able to slurp soup through a straw. I tell ya boyo, if me brothers were here, we'd have torn out his limbs and fed the bits to a starving kelpie!"

Unable to wrap his scientific brain around any of the leprechaun's insane rantings, Michael did the only thing he could think to do.

"I can't deal with this irrational behavior. You're... you're grounded!"

Biggleton's mouth dropped wide open, "I'm grounded?"

"Yes. Yes, you're grounded. I'm sorry, but you have to stay in this apartment. You have to do as I say, right?"

Before Biggleton could answer, Michael continued his rant. "You're making my head hurt. So, I'm going to bed. I need to be at work early. I have to figure out a way to prepare my colleagues and eventually the scientific community to learn of your existence. I'm sorry, Biggleton, but I'll be home at lunch tomorrow to check in on you. Unwind. Watch TV. Get some sleep. Just... don't get into anything."

Biggleton watched as Michael bit at a hangnail, pacing the length of the living room a few times until he finally scurried into the bedroom. Scratching his head, Biggleton plucked a lit pipe out of his pocket, held it between his teeth and pulled in deeply. He mumbled something in Gaelic under his breath and hollered for Michael.

"Hey, laddie. I believe you forgot to nick the beer."

When Michael left the apartment the next morning, Biggleton was curled fast asleep underneath the dining room table. He was terrified to leave the leprechaun, but he would come back from the lab sometime in the afternoon to check up on his guest and bring him something for lunch.

It was nearly 1:00 when Michael finally had a free moment to break away. He stopped at the deli around the corner from his apartment and grabbed two six-inch turkey subs and a bag of baked chips. He had calmed down considerably. "The little bum's probably still sleeping," he thought to himself.

As he made his way down the hall to his apartment, Michael's teeth began to rattle from the extreme bass pumping from one of the flats on his floor. Unexpectedly, the door to his apartment swung open, and a naked woman with huge breasts followed the music into the hallway.

"No, no, no!" Michael bleated, pulling off his jacket to conceal and shoo the woman back into his apartment without anyone noticing.

"Hey, you're kinda cute... for a dork," giggled the woman. "Come on in and join the party. It's craic! I just learned that today from a little Irish dude."

Steering her into the doorway, Michael locked the door behind him. Once inside he was immediately overcome by brash music and bright strobe lights. He thrust his way through a mob of strangers to find Biggleton supervising keg stands in the kitchen.

"I see you're home to join the fun, boyo. What have you in the bag?" he asked, snatching the plastic bag from Michael's wrist. "One bag of crisps and two puny sandwiches? If you haven't noticed, it's quite black in here. There ain't enough in this sack to keep that woman's monster diddies bouncing. Be a lad and fetch a bigger lot of grub."

Seizing the bag of snubbed food out of Biggleton's hands, Michael looked around in disbelief.

"Who are all these people and why are they in my house?"

At that moment, a keg stand participant tottered next to Michael, steadying himself using the scientists shoulder and vomited, showering Biggleton and Michael's shoes in beer and what looked like undigested eggs.

"On second thought" Michael shouted, "I don't care who they are. Get them out of my apartment! Now!"

Biggleton couldn't hear a word of it. He ripped off his faultlessly fashioned shoes and threw them at the sloppy drunk, hitting him in the groin.

"Never defile a pair of fine-crafted shoes!" He grabbed the hose from the keg and chugged. Coming up for air he growled "I'm gonna knack yer bollocks in!"

He lunged at the shoe violator, his tiny feet springing from the sullied ground but catching only air. Surprisingly, Michael caught him mid-attack by his pant legs and yanked him backwards, dumping Biggleton belly first on the tile.

"Whatcha gone and do that for and why are me balls feeling frosty?" Clenched in Michael's hand was the leprechaun's pants.

"Aye there, you slipped me out of me cacks! I always knew you were a poof. Hand 'em over, boyo."

Dumbfounded, Michael threw the tiny pants to the floor and picked his breast pocket for his cell phone. Disgusted and defeated, he ambled into the bathroom and phoned his lab manager. It seemed he wouldn't be in the rest of the afternoon.

After a few minutes of decompression, Michael splashed some cold water on his face and emerged from the bathroom. Waiting for him was a disturbing scene playing out in the living room. Biggleton had formed a posse and was flailing naked on the coffee table while the makeshift DJ turned up the volume. Biggleton and his adversary of a few minutes earlier now took turns with a beer bong, the shoe incident apparently forgotten. The music shifted from frenetic to full-on rap swagger, and the leprechaun broke into his own "gangsta rap":

You so tasty good,
I wanna lick your dishes.
You my lucky charm,
You magically delicious.

Michael decided the vulgar one-man show was over when one of the intoxicated groupies got a little too close to the action and was urged to 'kiss his Blarney Stones.' He grabbed a towel from the bathroom and wrapped it around the not-so-wee man before ushering him off of the coffee table to a barrage of boos, beer cups and chants of "release Lil' Biggie!"

Michael ushered him into a corner and pleaded with him. "Please, get these people out of here. I don't want to get thrown out of this apartment building. I'm a respected scientist, damn it. I've got too much to lose, so make them leave."

Biggleton's eyes were glazed over. Disinterested in Michael's pleas, he was instead fixated on a nude statuesque woman on the table. A cut crystal hung from her belly button ring, creating a rainbow when the sunlight from the kitchen window hit it just right. Gripping his shoulders, Michael gently tried to shake him free from his gaze. But the only thing that was shaken free was the towel.

Biggleton began to tremble as he approached the figure. His mouth gaped and drool dribbled from his lips. Michael reached for him but Biggleton was oblivious to anything else. His eyes never shifted from the light show sparked by the gaudy crystal dangling from the woman's navel. Realizing Biggleton had become paralyzed at the sight of the refracted light Michael raised his hand as if to shield the imp's eyes from the light and heartily slapped his face... twice. Eagerly, Michael raised his hand to slap him a third time but Biggleton caught his wrist.

"That'll be enough out of ya. If ya wanted 'em gone, why didn't ya just say so?"

He turned toward the living room and with a magical snap of his finger directed everyone to leave. As the party-goers slipped back into their clothes, one by one they walked out the door. Biggleton returned to the figurine in the kitchen.

"There ya go, boyo. I guess you've had enough fun for one day. I, on the other hand, have a few more things to attend to. Woman, where are you?"

"Thankfully, I think everyone is gone now, including your bare-breasted door greeter," chided Michael.

"Calm yourself, laddie. I didn't mean her." Biggleton reached for the figurine on the counter.

"I meant her." In his tiny hand was the bottle of Mrs. Butterworth syrup that had won his affection.

"She's a beauty like I've never seen," he said as he fondled her molded plastic breasts with his fat thumbs. "This may be the finest lassie my eyes have ever gazed upon. Say something, lassie. Don't play games with me heart."

Michael rolled his eyes. "I'm leaving you two alone." With that, he made his way for his bedroom. Exhausted and traumatized, he dropped to his bed to ponder his next move.

His eyes were closed but a few moments when he realized he was not alone in the bed.

"Biggie, is that you baby?" a semi-conscious voice responded.

"Dammit, I thought he threw everyone out. I'm afraid you've got to go," he shouted. As he flipped over the sheets, a horror unlike anything he had ever known greeted him.

"Oh, hey, sweetie. I know this is a little awkward but... next week, do you think you could come over and unclog the drain in the basement? You're so good at that stuff."

Michael's mother lay naked next to him, an empty shot glass in one hand and Biggleton's pipe in the other.

Michael's eyes popped wide open as he gasped for breath. It took a few minutes to realize it was only a dream. But the message was loud and clear. This Biggleton business was getting the better of him.

Michael knew Biggleton had to go. Although he was an extraordinary link between science and mythos, he needed that link to go somewhere else.

The original plan was purely scientific. Since he was the one who brought him into the corporeal plane, Michael had planned intense experiments on his own, which would eventually culminate with the big leprechaun reveal to his university board and ultimately, to the world. But Biggleton wasn't a force that would stay quiet and contained in order to provide Michael his chance to shine. He was, as Michael had noted in his journal, "a three-foot tall Category Five hurricane that relished wrecking everything in his path for pure indulgence."

Michael knew it was short notice to convene with the university's board of trustees and research staff to present his discovery, but it didn't matter. A gathering of his department chair and a few esteemed colleagues to see his discovery would have to suffice.

Michael quickly made a few covert phone calls while Biggleton remained in the kitchen. With his plans in place, he made his way to the living room, where he found Biggleton smoking his pipe while lying with the bottle of Mrs. Butterworth in his arms. He motioned to Michael for quiet, suggesting his new love had dozed off.

Michael again rolled his eyes. Ignoring Biggleton's wishes, he gathered some belongings with zeal.

"Well Lil' Biggie, since I can't trust you alone, we're going to the lab."

"That's a good bit of craic." Biggleton gently placed his towel over Mrs. Butterworth as a makeshift bed sheet. He quickly scanned the room and cringed.

"Ehhh... this place is an awful tip, don't cha think? I wouldn't take a piss in here."

Michael had gathered his colleagues into the conference room next to his laboratory. Biggleton sat center stage in a comfortable swivel chair, spinning and reveling in a euphoric head rush. Once everyone had settled in, Michael took his place beside what he referred to as "the 8th-and-a half wonder of the world" to present his findings.

"I want to thank you all for being gracious and granting me your time. I know you're all busy, but what I am about to reveal to you is truly a marvel for our modern world. Two days ago, while working with the spec prism, something I can only describe as unbelievable was brought forth into our plane of existence."

He took a deep breath and scanned the eyes of his audience. He seemed to have their full attention now.

"As a man of science, I am not one to accept the dalliances of myth and fairy tales. But science has now given credence to at least one such concept."

Michael nervously cleared his throat and abruptly ended the chair's fervent rotation. The abrupt stop tossed Biggleton from his seat onto the floor.

"Aye, ya arsehole, what'd ye go and do that for? I outta knock your pan in."

Glaring at the aggravated wee man picking himself off the ground, Michael quickly made his case.

"Okay, look, I can't believe I'm saying this myself. But ladies and gentleman... today... I present to you... a leprechaun. A leprechaun! Made tangible by my spec prism."

The room fell silent. No one said a word. But cynical expressions exchanged said more than words could. Michael's upper lip began to perspire.

"I understand your skepticism, but I'll prove it to you. Biggleton, show these respected doctors that you are indeed a leprechaun."

Producing the same cynical expression as his audience, Biggleton hopped back on the swivel chair and stroked his thickly whiskered chin.

"And just how do I do that, Michael? Do you think it states it on me driver's license? Do you expect me cacks to be brimming with shamrocks and gold? Oh, I know, you wish for me self to fart a rainbow? Well, why didn't ye say so?"

With that, Biggleton stood up on the chair, aimed his squat posterior towards his audience and feigned unbuckling his pants.

Clammy and enflamed with embarrassment, Michael stood between Biggleton's wiggling butt and his contemporaries, who were now snickering at the little man's antics. The exasperated scientist pulled Biggleton close and whispered in his ear.

"Come on, do something. Pull a lit pipe from your pants. Grant one of them a damn wish. Don't make me look like a fucking lunatic."

The imp hissed through his yellowed teeth. "You can't pawn me off on these eggheads that easily, boyo. I'm not done with ye yet. We're just starting to have a bit of craic."

Biggleton abruptly slipped a warm, slimy tongue into Michael's ear, then shoved him aside. Jumping from the chair onto one of the conference tables, he began strutting like a supermodel on a runway.

"Now everyone, in Michael's defense, for years little people have been stereotypically portrayed as leprechauns. And with his taking to the drink as of late, I really can't blame him for seeing little green men and pink elephants. Oh, he would have brought the pink elephant instead of me self, but it wouldn't fit in the elevator."

The room filled with laughter as Biggleton assumed a jig soaked in Irish tradition and dripping with mockery. Panicking for his credibility, Michael sprang to his self-defense.

"I'm not a drunk. He's making it up."

"Oh am I?" goaded Biggleton. "Well, then why do you carry a wee flask around in your lab coat pocket? What's it topped with, lemonade?"

All eyes were on Michael as he reached in his lab coat. A shiny flask etched with Michael's name was cradled in his hand. He threw it across the room.

"That's not mine. You put it there. I'm not a drunk. He's a damn leprechaun, a spiteful, son-of-a-bitchin' leprechaun."

Believing the joke had played out long enough, the scientists began to leave the conference room, patting Michael sympathetically on the back and heartily shaking Biggleton's hand. The department chair took Michael aside and asked to see him in his office at the end of the day.

Once everyone had filtered out, Michael charged from the conference room into his laboratory with the defiant leprechaun quick on his heels. Barricading the door behind him, Michael grabbed handfuls of small metal objects and emptied them in both coat pockets.

"I'm gonna kill you, you errant little bastard!" Michael swore as he lobbed horseshoes at the leprechaun's head.

One of the wayward horseshoes nicked the little leprechaun's reedy shin, toppling him over. Michael sprung on top of the wee man and pinned him to the cold laboratory floor. The glow from the leprechaun's yellow eyes dimmed.

"You've been doing your homework I see. We leprechauns aren't exactly fond of iron. Especially up our arse! But it ain't gonna kill us. Sorry about your luck!"

"I only gave you what you wished for, laddie," Biggleton proclaimed, amidst moans and yelps of pain. "So, please let me up from this foul parquet. I believe there's iron up my arse from those damned horseshoes." His pleas did little to loosen the grip the scientist had on him.

"Just look at yourself," he continued. "This isn't you, Mikey. You're not a killer. You're a man of science. Remember Mikey, you brought me into *your* life, and it has been nothing short of magical."

Michael jammed his knee in Biggleton's groin and snorted, "You ruined my life, you fucking prick." During the ruckus, a single coin escaped Michael's pant pocket. Michael noticed how the imp's eyes glazed over as the coin rolled under one of the desks and out of sight.

"Wait just a minute!" he said. Michael began to piece together an idea. Perhaps there was a better way to rid himself of his maddening infection.

Scrambling to his feet, he dug in his pockets and tossed a handful of change across the room, the coins bouncing from wall to wall under various machines, desks and chairs. Being true to his nature, the avaricious leprechaun canvassed the lab, scooping up every nickel, dime and penny. This gave Michael the time he needed to ready the machine that brought the wicked urchin into his existence in the first place. Hopefully it would be equally effective in sending him back.

"Woe to you, ya bastard, having filthied me! I'll eat your head cunt off!" Biggleton cursed as Michael snatched him up from behind while wriggling under a desk to nick a shiny quarter. Taking quite a few blows to the head and stomach from flailing arms and legs, Michael hauled his hostile quarry towards the glowing prism. The leprechaun's curses turned to pleas.

"Come on, Mikey, you know you don't wanna do this. Don't make me go into the light. Think of all the things I can do for ya. I can make things right with the university. I'll clean your apartment. Better yet, I'll make you rich, boyo. Rich. I'm the eighth-and-a-half wonder of the world, Mikey. Remember, science is your lady!"

Michael dug his fingers in the imp's arms and hissed in his ear.

"Science may be my lady, but just like any woman she can be a real bitch." With all the strength a scientist could muster, Michael tossed Biggleton into the machine's soft glow.

"Good riddance, ya little son of a bitch," he snapped, backing away from the effects of the prism.

The leprechaun squealed, "Ahh, the pain, the pain. Help me laddie, I'm melting. I'm melting." And with that, the leprechaun broke down in a fit of unnerving laughter.

"Hahahaha. I'm as sound as a lone wolf in a bucketful of sheep. Your little machine isn't blushing pretty enough to rid a soul like me." Biggleton gloated and danced a deranged jig in the light.

Biggleton was right. The machine wasn't as pretty as it had been two days prior. What was the catalysis? What was needed to reverse the effects?

Michael's thoughts raced at a maddening pace. The legends... leprechauns waiting at end of rainbows... that's what brought this creature here. The prism had refracted the light into its seven primary colors. The process had created a perfect rainbow, under perfect laboratory conditions.

"That's it, isn't it?" Michael asked of the leprechaun. "You never would have come here under perfect laboratory conditions. You're too smart for that. You knew you'd be caught under those conditions. But you... you thought this was nature. Why? What am I missing? What did I do to fool you into think..."

Michael hesitated for a second before remembering the one factor he had failed to reproduce from his first experiment. It had to be it.

"The *music*!" he proclaimed. "It was the music, wasn't it? The sound waves must have interacted with the light photons."

Biggleton's silence was answer enough. Racing towards the computer, Michael punched up the internet radio, called up a station titled Celtic Sounds and blasted it thru the lab. A panicked smirk slapped across the imp's lips.

"You think you're crafty, boyo? Well watch this." Raising a knee, Biggleton attempted stepping thru the refracted beams and was awarded with an electric jolt sending him reeling backwards.

"Turn it off, turn that cursed music off. You don't know what you're doing! You don't want to incur the wrath of a leprechaun. Evil death, short life to you, bastard!" he ranted.

The music was the catalyst. Just as it had two days earlier, the rainbow's splendor metamorphosed into a wall of sludge from the songs of the Emerald Isle. Michael cranked up the speakers. The muddy light waves violently shuddered, almost obscuring its prisoner behind it. With a thunderous grand finale, the machine exploded with a blinding light. As it dissipated, Michael scanned the room. There was no sign of the leprechaun. Biggleton was gone.

"The greatest scientific discovery of my generation," Michael said, "and I just may have to take it to the grave with me."

The planets had finally aligned in the magnificent Russian sky, just as Dr. Yuri Yakovlev had calculated. After years of diligence and millions of hard-earned grant rubles, the light spectrometer had been assembled, calibrated, and was now ready to be activated. Dr. Yakovlev initiated the machine's main boot sequence and perched himself at his computer. The light show was breathtaking. The son of accomplished symphony members, he felt it only appropriate to set this moment to some music. As he scanned his collection, he settled on his choice.

"Maybe some New Age/Celtic fusion would be appropriate," he declared.

A Perfect Eight

Numbers give a means of establishing scale and perspective. And while many of us aspire to dwell at the top of the scale, it's what happens just beneath the top—right below the water's surface—that is often more interesting.

"Dawny, order up on the live plate," the chef hollered as he slid the slithering dish through the window.

Despite her years of servitude to the family seafood restaurant, Dawn never ceased to be amazed by the number of diners who ordered the wriggling platter. Some considered themselves extreme diners who simply had to try the strangest foods on any menu. Some were braggadocios who would do anything on a dare. Sometimes even a foreigner would wander in, missing the comfort food from their homeland. The reasons never seemed to matter to her. This dish was most bizarre and yet surprisingly popular.

The "Live Plate" was aptly named. The tamest components were the oysters on the half-shell, their shells pried open and the soft meaty bodies scraped from their calcified mantle. The bivalves were accompanied by a small bowl filled with light broth, fragrant noodles and exotic dancing shrimp which often jumped from the dish onto the table (or floor, or laps) of customers, much to the entertainment of most everyone in close proximity. But center stage was the octopus, their eight legs twirled and grabbed on to the plate and oyster shells. To eat them properly, their boneless bodies were wrapped tightly around chopsticks and the diner tasked to swallow them whole without the suction cups attaching to their teeth, tongue and throats. This particular dish could result in suffocation and since death is never a positive dining experience, patrons signed a waiver before the meal could be served.

Dawn pried a desperate tentacle from her thumb as she delivered the live plate to a table of middle-aged men, each fueled by liquid courage and the desire to regain their youth and win the respect of their much younger girlfriends.

Dawn's older sister Nicole darted through the dining room to the kitchen, complaining to anyone within earshot. Among today's rants: her apron needing scrubbing this afternoon, and someone had stolen her pen and receipt pad. Dawn followed her into the kitchen.

"Nice of you to show up and grace us with your presence. And don't even think of pulling the tips on your tables when they leave, because they're mine. I did all the damn work."

Nicole pulled her compact mirror from her purse and carefully painted on a cotton candy smile.

"Oh, sister. Don't hate because I have a life outside of this hellhole," she said, grinning as she wiped the extra gloss from her perfect teeth. "And don't make me go through this again. I've only explained it like a million times now. *Moi* is a ten. And as a ten, I am afforded certain, uh, 'opportunities'. If those opportunities happen to get in the way of something mundane like serving seafood, then I need my supporting cast to pick up the slack. That's where the eights come in."

Fishing a rogue dancing shrimp from her apron pocket and flicking it at her sister, Dawn snipped back.

"And I've told *you* like a million times, I'm no eight."

"Of course you aren't," retorted Nicole. "You're more like a seven. But since you got rid of your disgusting back acne and started wearing contact lenses, I've elevated your status. You are my sister, after all."

Nicole rested her case by snacking on the shrimp Dawn had airmailed. Rolling her large hazel eyes, Dawn snickered.

"Elevated to an eight, huh?"

"A *solid* eight," Nicole corrected, picking shrimp legs from her teeth. "Oh, Dawny, you wouldn't want to be a ten. It's a curse. Boys are always asking you out. People want to do things for you and hang with you because you're so hot and popular. It's really tiring. I can't even keep up with my social networking. You don't wanna be a ten, trust me. It's better to be an eight than a ten."

"A solid eight, and don't you forget it, bitch," Dawn said with a grin. "And by the way, this solid eight isn't helping you close tonight. You're on your own. Oh and the table that just got their live plate needs more booze. Chop to it, 'your hotness'. Mamma needs a fat tip."

Nicole was again late for work the following afternoon. She flounced into the kitchen, and pinched her sister's arm.

"Dawny, did you hear what happened?"

"Did I hear that you're late *again* and that you're going to get fired?" Dawn snapped, ladling a bowl of lobster bisque. "No I didn't hear that, but it is some great news!"

"You wish, smart-ass. No, do you remember my table, the one that ordered the Live Plate? You know, the geezers and their gold-digger skanks—who were nines by the way?"

"You mean *my* table. And, yes, I remember them. How could I forget? They left me a shitty tip because someone forgot to refill their drinks, like I reminded them."

With an insincere, "Yeah, yeah, yeah," Nicole pulled her sister close, spilling a ladleful of bisque on the counter. "I thought I knew the chick with the great nose job and killer Jimmy Choos, but couldn't place her at first. Then I realized that she lives in my building. Or did, until an ambulance showed up and took her corpse out this morning. She's dead. Dead! Isn't that fucked up? I mean, they were just here last night. That is creepy. That's why I'm late. I wanted to make sure it was her they carried out of that apartment. I mean... what if it had something to do with our food?"

Dawn's eyes widened at the news, "Wow, that's just... wow. This restaurant is so clean you can eat off the floor. Aw, shit. Mom and Dad don't need this."

"It's probably just a weird coincidence. I mean... you can't get food poisoning that quickly, can you? Still, if anybody were to take the heat for something, it should be our fishmonger, Lin, not Mom and Dad. I've never liked that creepy old Asian freak in the first place. He's definitely a three, maybe a four at best." Nicole grabbed a rag to clean up the bisque, but threw it at Dawn instead.

"Lin is a sweet man. He's been hooking Mom and Dad up with the best fresh fish for years. He may be a little exotic, but the man has good stuff. The Live Plate was even his idea. And nobody's ever gotten sick from our food that we know of. So back off."

"Yeah." Nicole replied. "His stuff is killer. Get it?" Dawn chose to ignore the sarcasm and change the subject.

"Hey, I called you last night after work. Did you have a hot date or something? Did your phone die? I know you can't do anything without your phone smelling your rose scented farts in your ass-pocket."

Nicole paused, crossing her arms while trying to remember what she did last night. She knew she had been out with Mark the night before last. But that was where her memory seemed to hit a wall; she could not remember what she did last evening. Eventually, she shrugged her shoulders and shoved her pen in her tidily coiffed ponytail.

"I don't know. You and I had a beer at the end of shift. I went home and passed out because I was tired."

"How the hell were you tired? I did all your work!"

"Oh shut up, bitch, your Live Plate is up."

The restaurant's last patron was served and out the door by 10:00 P.M., and the door was locked by 10:10. Cleanup and restock for the next day took an additional hour. Finishing her work first, Dawn sat at the bar as she did after every evening stint and poured her shifty from the beer tap. Everyone employed at the restaurant was entitled to one draft after their shift. They called it their "shifty." Ten minutes later, Nicole joined her. Her shifty was patiently waiting for her on the freshly scrubbed bar. Dawn raised her glass, initiating a toast.

"To a job well done."

"You really want to toast to that? You're such a fucking... eight. How about this...'Here's to one day owning this joint and burning it to the ground for the insurance money.' Now that's a toast."

"You don't really mean that, do you?"

Nicole chugged her beer and let out an impressive belch.

"No. I just thought your toast was lame. But I don't want to work here the rest of my life. I have bigger aspirations than to smell like fish and make nice-nice to assholes so I can get a decent tip. This may be Mom and Dad's dream, but it ain't mine."

Dawn finished her beer and began washing their empty glasses.

"So what do you want to do? The position for Queen of England is already filled."

"I don't know. Something worthy of my curse, like fashion model or trophy wife for a millionaire. I look good in money."

"Yeah, well good luck with that," Dawn said, placing the glasses neatly on the drying rack.

"Well bitch, I gotta change and hose this stank off me. I have a date tonight with Mark, that yummy almost-lawyer. He's taking me dancing. Why don't you come with? I need someone to watch my purse while I'm out shaking my ass on the dance floor."

Dawn shook her head. "As enticing as that invitation may be, I have other plans. I told Mom I'd start inventory, and there's no time like the present. So have a good time, slut. Try not to contract genital warts. And don't be late tomorrow. I'm sick of doing your job."

"Yeah, whatever. Have fun being Mommy's little lap dog."

"Yo, ya worthless ho bag, get your ass up."

Dawn pounded on the door, alternating fists in a rhythmic beat. She had decided to make the several-block detour from her own apartment to her sister's in an attempt to make sure Nicole was not late for work again.

"This is your 2:00 P.M. wake up call. You're not going to be late again, so open the door and make me some coffee," she hollered loudly. Admitting defeat, she resorted to letting herself in with the key Nicole had given her in case of emergencies.

Once inside, she began a quick scan of the small apartment. Before she could make her way to the bedroom, she found her sister passed out on the bathroom floor. A handful of crumpled credit card receipts from the restaurant were scattered about. Dawn picked Nicole up and cradled her. She was dead weight, but she was breathing. After splashing handfuls of cold water on her face, Dawn gently shook her softly moaning sister.

"Nicole, open your eyes. Open your eyes. It's me, Dawny. Come on wake up. I'm not working by myself tonight or, worse yet, working with Edana. You know if I were to ever cut a bitch, it would be her."

Nicole's lips curled into a lazy smile. "You just hate her because she's an 8.5."

"That's it," Dawn laughed. "It has nothing to do with the fact that she's a lying whore with a bad boob job. You scared the hell out of me. What happened to you?"

Nicole leaned up against the cold porcelain of the bathtub. She tried to replay the previous evening in her head, but thinking just seemed to aggravate the pounding headache.

"I don't know. I was at work drinking my shifty, and then I'm lying on the bathroom floor with you slapping me. Dammit, you better not have left a mark. You know, I don't feel sick or anything, I just feel exhausted."

"Why don't you take the night off?" Dawn said, sifting through her purse for her cell phone. "I can call Kriste. I think she's off today and could use the extra cash."

"Right," Nicole scoffed. "I'll call off, and have you tell Mom and Dad I'm irresponsible and a light weight. I won't give you the satisfaction. Put on a pot of coffee. This bad bitch is going to kick some seafood ass tonight."

Nicole made her way to her feet and started a hot shower. As Dawn made her way to the kitchen to brew some coffee, Nicole shouted over the steaming waterfall.

"And by the way thanks for checking on me. And Edana isn't an 8.5. I was just screwing with ya."

"Hey chicks, did you hear what happened to Dirty Dean?" Edana asked in a whisper, as Dawn and Nicole tied their aprons and filled the pockets with straws and mint candies. Both girls shrugged, uninterested in yet another news flash from Edana. Her relationship with a police officer came with a few perks, including recounts of happenings from the night shift. And she reveled in playing the role of news anchor the next day.

The girls were particularly disinterested in any news on Dean Kush, a.k.a. 'Dirty Dean', a handsome but contemptible regular who happened to be a former high school classmate of Nicole's. His unhealthy appetite for exotic seafood, coupled with his stories about exotic sexual escapades, was enough to turn off everyone but his inner circle of equally eccentric friends.

The disregard for her blather didn't hinder Edana from continuing. In fact, she barely paused for air.

"So, Tony comes home this morning and tells me he got called to Dirty Dean's place last night. His roommate found him dead! They're still trying to figure out what fucked him... literally. I bet he tried to have sex with the octopus from the live platter he ordered last night and it tore his dick off. Didn't you wait on him, Nicole?"

Both girls were stunned, abandoning their bogus task of apron stuffing.

"Just what are you trying to say?" asked Nicole.

Edana smirked, "Nothing, girl. I just know how he used to try and charm you every time he'd come in. Now you can use your tits to suck the tips out of some other poor bastard's wallet."

Getting in Edana's face, Nicole hissed.

"A man is dead, Edana. How can you be so callous?"

"Easy, Nicole. I didn't give two shits about that disgusting prick. I mean, I'm sorry the guy's dead. But he was a waste of gorgeous man meat if you ask me. When someone eats the same shit he screws, something nasty is bound to happen." Edana's frank rant was cut short by the bellowing of the chef.

"Edana, order up, table twelve." The girls glared at her as she kicked open the swinging door to deliver the table's dinner.

"God, I can't stand her," Dawn said as she whipped a handful of sugar packets in Edana's direction. "She's probably just pissed because Dirty Dean wouldn't stuff her calamari."

Nicole was quiet, a little too quiet. She never passed on the chance to talk smack on anyone, especially Edana. Noticing her sister's mood had changed, Dawn attempted to make light of the situation.

"I'll be back. I don't think she washed her hands before she left the kitchen. I may have to remind her of that... in front of her customers. I'll kick that stupid bitch in the pocket book."

Dawn followed after her unwary prey. Leaning against the stainless-steel counter, Nicole's mind raced. She wondered why she could not remember the events of the previous night, before waking on the bathroom floor. Carefully, she replaced the receipts she didn't remember stealing and prayed no one noticed. Scribbling on her order pad, she then added one more to the pile. Nicole had found the original chewed up and crushed in her fist when she came to on the floor.

1 carafe of white wine, cod milt appetizer, live plate, 89.80 paid cash, Dean Kush.

After a tense shift, Nicole skipped her usual shifty with her sister and went straight home to digest the recent events. She told herself it was a bizarre coincidence. She could not have had anything to do with the deaths of Dirty Dean or her neighbor. She could not think of one explanation for how she could be involved, or one reason why she would be. But the other possibilities were almost as disturbing. What if it was her parent's restaurant, or old man Lin's food? She was embarrassed to admit it, but she actually hated the thought of losing her job if the place was shut down. After an hour of tossing and turning in bed, she finally melted into the inviting confides of sleep.

Nicole awoke the next morning with an initial bit of apprehension. She remained in bed for a few minutes, as if running some sort of a systems check. A quick scan of the room confirmed she was indeed in her bedroom. She was in possession of her memories from the night before, from the obnoxious encounter with Edana to Dawn's attempt at revenge. Confident that all was normal and that her fears from last night were irrational, she peeled off her covers. After making a turkey sausage and egg white omelet, she decided it would do her good to do get out of the apartment a bit before heading to the restaurant. She slid on her "shopping shoes" and headed out to the nearby shopping district. Ten minutes before her shift was to start, Nicole strolled into the restaurant showing off a new pair of tasteful sterling silver drop earrings. She felt good. She began her shift on a high note, earning her a few generous tips in return for her unusually pleasant demeanor. Her mood quickly faded at the sight of Mark, who was seated at one of her tables alongside an attractive blonde. Dawn noticed the tension in her sister's face and offered assistance.

"What's with the stink eye? You want me to take the table? I'll spit in their food for ya."

"That's Mark," Nicole bristled. "I have no clue what to say to him about the other night. I don't remember a damn thing after I left here. Maybe we went dancing and had a great time and I just don't remember it."

"Something tells me that's not the case," replied Dawn, giving her sister an incredulous look. "If you haven't noticed, Botox Barbie is glued to his dick."

"She *would* have to be a nine," Nicole replied. "Even though I don't remember what happened the last time, I do remember what happened earlier in the week. I can accurately describe the dick that naughty nine is glued to. Maybe she should find out. Stand back... this could get ugly."

Slipping the pen from her ponytail, Nicole sauntered to their table with a grin on her face. And within minutes she stormed back in the kitchen. Dawn raced to her side.

"So what happened? Did you bust him?"

"The bastard acted like he didn't know me. He even called me ma'am! That arrogant cocksucker."

"Get the hell out of here" Dawn spat. "I can't believe he disrespected you like that. "He ordered the crabs, didn't he? Well, by the looks of his date he's gonna get those whether he wants them or not later tonight. Speaking of, what was the prima donna Barbie's selection? Let me guess... Lobster Pot?"

"Yep, the pretentious cunt." Nicole seethed as she threw the order slip at the chef.

"And his order?"

Nicole angrily snatched an octopus from the tank and threw it on the large oval platter.

"Live Plate."

Dawn awoke to the sound of Rick James singing "Super Freak." Shaking off enough of her slumber to realize it was the ring tone she recently assigned to Nicole, she reached for her cell.

"Dammit Nicole it's 3:30 in the mor..."

Nicole interrupted Dawn before she could finish her complaint.

"Dawny, please help me. I'm at Mark's house. Mark's girlfriend is dead. I... I think I killed her."

When Dawn arrived, she found her sister huddled in the corner of the bedroom in a fetal position. The woman she had earlier labeled a "Naughty Nine Botox Barbie" was naked and spread-eagle on the bed. Her mouth hung open in a voiceless scream, while her eyes bulged as if focused on an assailant.

Dawn attempted to quickly survey the situation. There were no marks on the woman. Not a bruise, a cut, or drop of blood. But there was no mistaking her for anything but dead. Mark lay next to her. He was unconscious, but Dawn determined that he was still breathing. Careful not to touch anything, Dawn lifted her quivering sister from the corner and wrapped her in a black robe, grabbed from the bathroom. Dawn gently closed the bedroom door and the two guardedly made their way out of the house and headed toward Nicole's apartment.

Neither spoke a word until they were safely locked behind the apartment door. Collapsing on the living room floor Nicole whimpered.

"I don't remember anything. I don't know how I got there. Jesus, I think I'm going crazy."

Dawn slumped on the floor next to her. She pulled the robe tightly around her sister.

"What *do* you remember?"

"I remember closing up. I remember counting tips while we drank our shifties. I remember walking towards my apartment door and then... nothing. Nothing! It's all blank until a few seconds before I called you." Her body began to tremble violently.

"Oh my God, what if he saw me? What if he saw me? Fuck, what did I do?"

Dawn grabbed her sister's face in her hands. She took a deep breath to collect her own thoughts.

"Calm down. We're gonna figure this out. But you've got to keep calm. You can't draw any unwanted attention to yourself. You're off for the next two days, so lay low. But go about your daily routine. Don't give anyone reason to suspect you of anything. We'll get through this. I promise."

In the days that followed, Nicole did her best to follow her sister's advice and keep as low a profile as her lifestyle allowed. But the fear of a SWAT team bursting through the restaurant door every time it swung open caused enough anxiety to send her home twice from panic attacks. Keeping to her routine outside of work was not a real option. Nicole finished her chores and hurried home, bolting the door behind her before spending her evenings in a sleepless state of floor-walking.

Edana was soon able to provide her usual Tony-fed update. Mark had been brought in for questioning. The news somewhat assuaged Nicole's dread, but began gnawing away at her conscience. She was not sure if she could live with herself should an innocent man pay for her crimes. Even more confounding to her was the question of what happened. For all she knew, Mark might be guilty after all.

The Saturday night rush helped to improve Nicole's spirits. She found it easier to hold her anxieties at bay as long as she was running down tables and orders. An hour before closing, a small group of Nicole's close friends showed up and took a seat at her station. She felt it was just what she needed to feel somewhat normal again. Attractive enough to be models, the small clutch of females and one lone male were raucous and energetic, owed to a few rounds of alcohol. Nicole rushed over to them.

Dawn watched her sister laugh and carry on with her friends. She recognized two of them from high school. The lone male in the group was Peter Hayes, who had been an all-city basketball star. But Dawn had always found him to be a stereotypical obnoxious jock. It appeared he was still dating the former cheerleader who deemed Dawn and her friends "the untouchables." The couple harassed Dawn and her friends throughout high school, and even helped Nicole develop the rating system that she remained so fond of to this day. As Dawn watched and reflected, she remained exasperated that Nicole would remain friends with such a group.

Despite her angst, Dawn took up the slack and began serving Nicole's tables. Walking by the boisterous group, Dawn heard Peter call out to her.

"Hey, how about a drink over here? Your sister's visiting with us!"

"So you're gonna sit there and get sloppy ass drunk?" Dawn retorted, no longer able to refrain from a confrontation. She chose her next words carefully.

"You know, you really should eat something. I recommend the Live Plate. A big man like you should have no problem wrestling your dinner, unless you're a pussy."

Like a mother embarrassed of her ill-mannered child, Nicole immediately responded.

"What the hell, Dawn?"

"Well," Peter retorted, "all these ladies here at the table can tell you I'm no pussy."

Dawn scribbled down the order, "So you'll have the Live Plate? Oh, and by the way, they say it's an aphrodisiac. After all those drinks you sucked down, you may need a little help this evening if you plan on throwing it to your, um... lady."

"Dawn!" snapped Nicole, before following her into the kitchen. "What's the matter with you? Why are you being such an ass to my friends?"

"Because your friends are asses," Dawn replied as she handed the chef the order.

"Well, fuck you. Those are my friends. Like I haven't been through enough already this week, now I have to deal with your behavior? You know what? I'm done for the night. You and Edana can close up." Nicole threw her apron to the floor in protest.

"I really don't think so," Dawn snipped.

"And why the fuck not?" Nicole yelled as she kicked her apron.

Snatching the order in the window and shoving it at her sister, Dawn smirked. "Because the Live Plate is up for your table."

The end of the night was met with silence. Both girls completed their respected chores, carefully avoiding one other. After egging Peter on through completion of his Live Plate, Nicole's friends had left without further incident—save for a few trips to the bathroom thanks to the cocktails and the sight of Peter ingesting the live octopus. Dawn poured her shifty and sat at the bar next to Edana. Nicole grabbed her tips and started out the door.

"Woah, where you going in such a hurry, girly?" asked Edana as she wiped the foam of her own shifty off of her lips.

Without looking back, Edana yelled "I'm going home to get dressed... and then I'm going to party with my *friends*."

Nicole found the porch light on and the back door open, so she let herself in. She was greeted by top-40 music blaring from the next room. She yanked open the thick wooden pocket doors into the dining room.

"Hey guys, I made it!"

Taking only a few steps through the dimly lit room, she tripped and fell face-forward onto the hardwood floor.

"Aww... son of a bitch," she groaned. The groans turned to laughter as she realized that her stumble was the result of a trip over one of her friends, who also lay flat on the floor.

"You can't be that wasted already. Come on and get up. I'm here to get this party started."

Nicole tried propping her friend up, but found the task a tall order. The girl hung limp.

"Fuck. Fuck, wake up. Come on!"

Nicole started to panic. The events of the past week began again to play on her mind.

"Somebody get in here and help me!"

The loud music faded. A familiar voice took center stage.

"I can help you, but there's no help for her. I suppose I can at least leave her the way I found her. Here, kitty kitty..."

Nicole barely stifled a scream as the mouth of her friend was forced open by eight serpentine arms that protruded from within. A supple body slid from between her dead lips, and slid its way into Dawn's hand.

"No one appreciates these creatures. They're cunning. They're intelligent. They're deadly. They're beautiful, and most people do not see the beauty. In fact, most people do not give them a second thought. They are what you might call an '8'. Just like me."

"What are you talking about, Dawn? What is going on? What did you do?" Nicole remained frozen, mesmerized at the invertebrate clinging to her sister like a child to its mom.

"So damn pretty, but so dense. Typical for a 10. Here, have a seat next to your friends at the table. They are your friends, right?"

Dawn yanked a chair out from under the table, jostling the flaccid body of the ex-jock from his perch. His head cracked open as it smashed on the sharp corner of the table before he hit floor next to Nicole.

"Oh my God, what the fuck, Dawn?" As Nicole's eyes adjusted to the dim light, she noticed her two other friends slumped on the table.

"My, this does look like a fun party. But you need explanations, no doubt. Just let me scare up the rest of my friends."

With that, Dawn pursed her glossed lips and let out a jarring whistle. Twirling tentacles darted from the slack jaws of the dead while Dawn sweetly reassured them there was nothing to fear. The small army of color-shifting octopi wriggled towards the promising sound of her voice, slinking one by one into a cooler full of chilly saline.

"Remember when you told me being a '10' was a curse, and that I should be happy being an '8'? It made me feel terrible. Grotesque. No one should exist feeling that way. So if being a ten is such a burden, then it's only right that I should take it away from you. It's the least a sister can do."

As Dawn stroked the mantle of the octopus still clinging to her fingers, the creature seemed to respond to her every move. She smiled approvingly and continued her explanation.

"I've grown up in your shadow, sis. All of my life I've watched you get the attention that only beauty brings. I could have lived with it, if I didn't have to hear about your stupid rating system all the time. It wears on a girl. It keeps her up at night. One night in particular. On that night, I decided to take a walk. Soon I found myself on the docks, near Lin's place. And the old man was there too, doing whatever it is old fishermen do."

Nicole continued to stare in horror. It was as though the Dawn she grew up with was replaced with a stranger.

"I learned a few things that night Nicole. I learned that Lin thought of us as family. I learned that the old man is more than a fish salesman. I learned that he dabbled in *kuromajutsu*, Japanese black magic. And once I told him I was hurting after a lifetime of feeling inferior, he taught me a few things. He showed me how to use *kuromajutsu* to capture beauty from another.

"Dawn, have you lost your mind?" Nicole cried. "What are you talking about?"

131

Undaunted, Dawn continued.

"He taught me to pick any creature, and compel that creature do the work for me. The work needed to send my spirit into another's body. I chose the octopus to serve me. You do get the irony, don't you? It has eight legs. *I'm* an 8. I've been serving them up to customers for years. It is a beautiful creature that the world sees as something less than beautiful. Which is how I have felt all of my life. These creatures are my soul mates. Even you have to admit that."

"Dawn, listen... whatever I did to make you freak out like this... I'm so sorry."

Dawn ignored her sister as she continued. Her attention was squarely on the creature wrapped around her arm.

"Lin taught me how to perform the spell. And guess what? It worked! The whole thing worked. They did my bidding. All I needed was a weak spirit, and her beauty was mine for the taking. I will never be an 8 again. I will never be less than perfect. I am a 10."

Dawn finally acknowledged her sister's presence again. She turned to her trembling sister, still huddled on the floor.

"But Dawny... you look the same. You've killed everyone and you're the same. Whatever crazy Japanese magic shit you think you pulled, it didn't work. All you've done is kill a bunch of innocent people!"

"Sister, the 'crazy Japanese magic shit', as you put it, is only half the equation. Lin said I needed a weak spirit to inhabit the body. You fucking 10's might be dumb as logs, but you're not weak. You've got spunk. So I had to take a few things into my own hands. I had to drug a shifty. I had to make someone believe that they were capable of murder. I had to make someone question their own sanity. Someone who I've always wanted to be, all of my life."

As the octopus leapt toward Nicole, Dawn began reciting the spell. She paused long enough to offer a final few words.

"Goodbye, sis. I promise to take good care of your body. I'll sleep in every day and get others to do my work. Oh, and I've already implicated the old me for the Botox Barbie's death, so no worries about Mark rotting in jail. In fact, I promise to take real good care of him. I've always had a mad crush on him. I think he's going to like the new you."

As Dawn stepped into Nicole's car, she took a look at her new reflection in the rearview mirror.

"Nicole, we've got a lifetime of fun to catch up on. And technically, it's my 'birthday'. So, let's get started."

Revolution Nine

Numbers permeate nearly every facet of our lives, and have even carved a space in pop culture. Numeric references appear in theater and song. Most of us probably fail to give such uses more than a passing interest. But what if their presence means much more that it may seem?

His head was small. Much smaller than the aggressive Floch Heads that cruised through space. His slender body, hidden underneath a 'haute-couture' floor length snood was the color of the inside of a cucumber and just as cool and slick. Dobra extended his long tendrils and bowed to his queen, waiting for her to return his touch before he spoke. She coiled her rhizome-like fingers around his, giving him the permission he desired.

"Your Highness, we have successfully taken over Planet Facio 54. They have released their hierarchy and opened their airspace to us. At the Aurora Rising 2300, the entire race pledged allegiance to the Empire. We have a fleet of ships en route. They will be ready to colonize within the 5-moon orbital shift."

"That is glorious news, Dobra!" Queen Noid squealed. "Let this teach the Flochs that brute force does not always win wars or expand territories. With a little patience, ingenuity, and mind softening, entire worlds can be infiltrated and toppled from within. If I've said it once, I've said it a sextillion times... win their culture, and you win their world."

The opportunity to again lecture her views on conquering worlds brought her toothless mouth to a smile that expanded the entire width of her face. She enunciated each word slowly in her native tongue of Svoglovian, in a condescending manner meant to stress her superior intelligence over her underlings.

"As my dear momo always said, 'invasion doesn't need to be bloody, it just needs to be irresistible," she continued.

"Let the Flochs have their bloodbaths; our victories will reap greater rewards."

"It was an ingenious idea to use the Facite's vanity as their undoing," conceded Dobra. "You are a wise and shrewd Monarch. Tell me, my Queen, what was the inspiration for the snoods of mood-altering colors?"

"It was quite ingenious, wasn't it, Dobra? But a queen does not reveal all of her fashion secrets. Exactly how long after the ninth revolution did the planet collapse?"

Dobra punched up the ship's log for review on the big screen. "From Revolution 1 and the introduction of the fashionable functional snood, through Revolution 9 and the financial collapse, it took 4500 clicks after the Aurora Delta Waning to overtake the snood-obsessed people. Not quite as quickly as the Planet Caskcar, where nine revolutions were reached in a mere 800 clicks. Thank Hasskala for the Caskcarian's love of Mamoochas."

"Mamoochas!" the queen snorted. "I had almost forgotten about those repulsive snot-stuffed creatures. Who would have thought tossing them in oil and dousing them in Loo sauce would cause the Caskcarians to gorge themselves right out of a planet? Oh wait, I did."

Both Svoglovians laughed, entwining their creamy white tendrils in a Svoglovian version of a "high-five." Remembering his place in the hierarchy, Dobra retracted his appendages and nobly addressed his queen.

"It is a testimony to the greatness of your leadership and the perfection of your methods. You have once again shown us that we can conquer any world in nine steps, each causing a revolution from within. In a mere nine revolutions, you take any world you like. One thing I still fail to understand, though. I beg your forgiveness for my ignorance, but... why nine?"

"Much of this is beyond your understanding, Dobra," lectured the Queen. "But I have learned that every living species has an exposure threshold. Some will succumb to something new after one generation is exposed. But one is rarely enough for any species capable of higher order thinking. One is fine for mamoochas, but few others. Across the galaxy, time and time again, it has been proven. Nine generations of exposure makes something permanent. Nine revolutions. No species can withstand nine."

"Which begs the question: what is your next conquest, my Queen?"

Almost giddy, Queen Noid flipped a bulbous flashing switch on the ship's console. A huge mirror and spinning 'disco ball' descended from the ceiling. Snatching a glowing baton usually reserved for torture, the queen struck a flamboyant pose, singing into her makeshift microphone.

"Eaaarthhhh."

"We will be arriving on planet Earth in 20 clicks. This will be my greatest conquest," she said to a core group of Svoglovian soldiers who were busy researching Earth's history and current culture. "Earthlings are fascinated with music. So, we will soften their minds by creating a new form of music, a whole new genre designed to prepare the lower life forms for domination. Our scouts have already preceded us, and have laid the groundwork and planted the musical seeds."

"I am particularly excited for this invasion because, as you all know, music is a passion of mine. And as you also know, my vocal abilities trump those of any life form throughout the universe. So it only makes sense, that I, your Queen, implant herself at the climax of Revolution 9."

The soldiers' bean-sized green eyes darted back and forth in disbelief and terror. Dobra, who was standing next to his Queen, shot a silencing glare to each one. But he knew and understood exactly what was running through their minds. Each undoubtedly was thinking that the Queen's singing voice sounded like a live mamoocha shrieking while being deep fried. But, as ruling monarch, Queen Noid's whims and "talents" were catered to and, unfortunately, encouraged.

Encouraging her singing was harmless when it merely meant wincing through some high notes. But with a planetary conquest riding on every move, Dobra felt he had to speak up. He chose his words carefully.

"My Queen, have you thought this through? Do you wish to put yourself in harm's way? If something were to happen to you, I could never live with myself. Besides, who would lead us?"

Noid wrapped a tendril around one of his. He took an apprehensive stance, unsure if the ulterior motive for his objection was a little too obvious.

"Nonsense, Dobra", Noid said. "This is what I was *born* to do, for the perpetuation of my race. I acknowledge your concern, but do not worry. This will be my moment of triumph, and I want to be at the front and center of it. Not only as your queen, but as your greatest soldier. The ultimate conquest, led by the grandest of rulers. They shall speak of this in every corner of the galaxy." Slapping her tendrils, she called for one of her warriors.

"Stand before me, brave soldier. You are next. You have been briefed and you are ready. The time has come. Take possession of the body, and launch the next revolution. Be brave; the host is grotesque, but our greatest minds are convinced this will be a popular figure, especially among the females. Remember your training. Remember the moves. You were chosen because of your gimpy hips. These humans are attracted to physical moves—the primeval perverts. Like the mating dances of the Cordivians. Lastly, make certain you use the toilet before you are inserted into the human. You will not be able to go again until the body's failure. Elvis, make the Svloglovians proud."

The revolutions had escalated in less than 550 clicks, almost two decades in Earth time. The Svloglovians were impressed with the human mind and its ability to be influenced and molded so quickly. Growing more excited about her installation into the upcoming revolution, the Queen requested a briefing of the previous revolutions. She grilled the soldiers assembled in the conference room, each masquerading uncomfortably in their human forms.

"Bring me up to speed. Hectid, now known as 'Bob', we'll start with you. Give me your report. How goes it?"

With that, Bob picked up his guitar and began singing.

"Well. The people and times... they are a' changing. They all enjoy smoking these cigarettes that make your hookpeepers feel funky while it's all blowin' in the wind. Let me wrap my human lips around this Svloglovian sexual device or as 'the Man' calls it, a harmonica. It'll make you understand it better, ya dig?"

Dobra tore the harmonica from Bob's headpiece.

"You will not disrespect the Queen by spelooching into a filthy hoggaholer. James. James? Please come forward and address your Queen. James? Where is the one renamed 'James'?"

Bob spoke up, "He couldn't make it."

The Queen's tiny black bean-shaped eyes widened to the size of kidney beans. "Explain!"

Strumming his guitar, Bob sang, "Weeeell, Jim snarfed some L-S-D. He said something about not being able to commune with you today because of some door. Then he started reading some poetry. I cried."

Seeing the fury in the Queen's beady little eyes, Dobra stopped the performance. "Unacceptable! This mission is not for your gratification."

Turning to the Queen, Dobra continued. "I am sorry, Your Majesty, for this insolence. But there is some good news. We are ready for Revolution 8."

The Queen's eyes softened. "Splendid. I must prepare."

Bob launched into another song:

Once upon a time you dressed so fine
But you didn't hide your spacecraft worth a dime,
didn't you?
You better hide it from the men in black.
Before they discover us and bust this cat.
It will be hard when we're discovered and we're
scrounging for our last meal.
How does it feel?
To be on your own.
With no direction home.
Like a rolling stone.

"I just wrote that. It's gonna be a hit one day."

Unmoved at the harbinger's song, the Queen quickly delivered orders.

"Revolution 8 will now begin. My chosen soldiers, prepare yourselves for emergency insertion. Dobra, we must move the ship to a secure location. We will contact you when we are certain we cannot be compromised. And warriors, remember: everything we have accomplished here on Earth is depending on you. Your names will go down as heroes in the Svloglovian historical tomes. You are the chosen ones. You are my fab four."

The scruffy radio DJ tried his best to do the job at hand, but his nerves kept getting the better of him. He was, after all, basking in the grandiosity of the world's biggest band. He took a puff of his cigarette and tried to calm his nerves before proceeding.

"So... 'Revolution 9'. That's one hell of a crazy song, man. Just what are you cats trying to say? Are you protesting the war in Vietnam? Are you speaking out for civil rights? Your fans across the airwaves are dying to know."

John, who had smoked a freshly rolled spliff before the interview, leaned toward his microphone, attending to his own job at hand.

"Everyone should listen to that song again and again to comprehend every little nuance and every drop of tone. You need to open your heart and the song will expand your soul. And soften your minds."

The other band mates gasped at John's frankness. The one dubbed Ringo interrupted before John could reveal anymore.

"What John is trying to say is that the song has layers. Listeners need to peel back those layers to immerse themselves in the music's resonance and dissonance and, and... sustenance."

The DJ sat slack-jawed in his chair, absorbing every word that spilled from their British-accented lips.

"Wow man, that's deep." His confidence growing, he now turned to bigger topics. "There's a rumor I'm sure you are aware of. A growing circle of fans believe that the 'real' Paul was killed, and has been replaced by a double. This is allegedly alluded to in 'Revolution 9'. It's not helping the argument that only three of you are here today in the studio. Is the cryptic message true? Is Paul dead?"

It was now the band's turn to be nervous. John and George shot a glance toward Ringo, the commander of this squadron and the only sober one sitting for the interview. He had been sent as a replacement when the original commander failed to corral the team and their partying ways. As this interview looked ready to unravel, he feared he was having no more luck than his predecessor. Before he could intercede, a baked John once again spoke up.

"Just like the song said, Russ, Paul is dead. He died in a horrific car accident. It tore off his head and left him... sans head. They tried to piece him back together, but half of him was inside out. All six of his arms were torn off. One of them ended up in a lizard's belly. The little wanker wouldn't give it up. It's all in the song, man."

Shocked again by John's candid commentary, Ringo dropped his head on the desk. The sound of the thud reverberated through the studio.

His confidence now soaring, the DJ played along with what he felt was the band's attempts to entertain the audience.

"This is a sad, sad day in rock history, my friends. Our hearts are heavy. We're all gonna miss him."

"Well, not me," John interrupted. "Nobody likes him but his momo. Fortunately we can have a replacement ready overnight. This chap will be much more agreeable. Of course, we'll call him Paul, too."

George began to giggle uncontrollably

"Is it... is it Paul, too? Or Paul Two?" holding up two fingers. "I love mushrooms," he added.

"I think you need to play the song again, for Paul," John said.

"There you have it, pussy cats. Straight from the band's mouth, Paul is indeed dead. A sad, sad day." The DJ continued on, in an Orson Wells War-of-the-Worlds-like manner.

"I'll leave you weeping gently with your guitar for 'Revolution 9'."

Just as Russ the DJ was placing the needle on the record, the studio door swung open. It was Paul, looking like he had just returned from the battlefields in Viet Nam. His eyes were black and blue and his face and hands had scrapes and cuts in different stages of healing. His shaggy hair looked crooked on his head, like it was stapled on.

"Which one of you bloody wankers locked me in the loo?" he said, clearly agitated. A small ticker tape parade of toilet paper clung to his loafer, celebrating the occasion.

"Paul is back from the dead; he's the ghost of shits past!" said George as he fell from his chair onto the floor, laughing like a deranged clown.

"Oh, bugger," John moaned under his breath. "He's not dead."

Paul looked at his band mates in disgust. "You're bloody right I'm not dead."

Russ laughed out loud. "Man, you guys are fun. Hey, what do you think the Queen Mum would think of this little stunt? You think she's got a sense of humor?"

With that, the room felt silent. Paul looked to his mates and said, "The Queen. The Queen is going to kill us when she hears about your nonsense. She'll scorch our ninnesas and rip off our bangers."

The DJ snickered, "You Brits sure do have some funny sayings, and a particularly far-out sense of humor. Do you have anything to say to your adoring fans before you split?"

George whisked the microphone from the desk, almost unplugging it, and whispered, "Obla-dee. Obla da. Life goes on. Just not always the way you expect it. And most importantly, I love shrooms."

Pumping his fist in the air, Russ murmured, "Right on man. Right on."

"Revolution 9 has failed."

Dobra broadcast the news throughout the mother ship as he instructed his crew to ascend from the depths of the ocean floor in the Baltic Sea.

"If we do not evacuate now, our location will be compromised by maritime fortune hunters. We must retreat, or they will descend upon us in numbers too great for us to repel."

Panicked, one of the soldiers reminded Dobra of their loyalty to the Queen.

"What of our Leader? What of our Queen? She has been inserted for 16784 clicks and has integrated into the human culture. They revere her as a song bird. She shines like a radiant star."

Dobra closed his tiny eyes, "Our plan has been undone by its own creator. Queen Noid is lost to us. Her quest for stardom was too great. Her style was unable to put a nail in the deathbox of this species. In fact, so weak are their minds that her musical tirades only distracted them from our purpose."

"Furthermore, she is happy with this. Our people are no longer her priority. If we do not retreat, we will be captured. We cannot take that risk. The duty now falls on me to bring any Svloglovians who wish to return back with us. For the sake of our race, let us go and reevaluate our failure here on Earth."

Staring out the window as the craft burned through the atmosphere, Dobra listened to a few final broadcasts from the planet's surface, musings from a show in the city of Las Vegas:

Near, far
Wherever planet you are
I believe that your three hearts do
Go on...

"I knew you should not have gone there, my Queen. Why did you not heed my advice? Your adoring crowds cannot love you as we did. But I know you now live your dream."

Dobra turned down the volume, wincing and recoiling at the sound of the Queen's vocals. As the space craft lifted higher and higher into the black abyss, the signal became dim.

"So close," thought Dobra. "Eight revolutions. We had them right where we wanted them. But everything backfired. You said it once before. No species can withstand nine revolutions. Not even ours. We got just as caught up in it as our conquests did. The fame, the riches... and those mushroom things. It felled the one sent as 'Elvis.' It felled your

143

'Fab Four'. And it destroyed us while it was working to destroy the Earthlings. And the death blow? You, my Queen.

"Your own delusions of grandeur and dreams of musical acclaim were too easy of a target. Your 'style'—or lack thereof—broke the Earthlings of the spell we had them under. Your own plan backfired on you. Now you are one of them, seeking only the spotlight. Now your chants undo the damage our 'rock and roll' had done. Nine revolutions were simply too much for you.

"You were right. It is the same across the galaxy." With that, his extraordinarily- wide mouth burst into a smile.

"Good bye and good luck, Queen Celine 'Dion'. You are going to need it."

About the Author

Ruschelle Dillon

Ruschelle Dillon is a freelance writer whose efforts focus on the dark humor and the horror genres. Ms. Dillon's brand of humor has been incorporated in a wide variety of projects, including the irreverent blog *Puppets Don't Wear Pants* and novelette "Bone-sai", as well as the live-action video shorts "Don't Punch the Corpse" and "Mothman". She also interviews authors for the *Horror Tree* website.

Her short stories have appeared in numerous anthologies and online zines.

Ruschelle lives in Johnstown with her husband Ed and the numerous critters they share their home with. When she isn't writing, she can be found teaching guitar and performing vocals and guitar in the band Ribbon Grass.

Stalk her on-
https:www.ruschelledillon.blogspot.com/
https://www.facebook.com/ruschelle.dillon
https://www.amazon.com/Bone-Sai-Ruschelle-Dillon-ebook/dp/B0088D275C
https://www.amazon.com/Strangely-Funny-III-Kevin-Wetmore/dp/0996420967
https://www.amazon.com/Weird-Ales-2-Another-Round/dp/1540303403
https://www.amazon.com/Women-Horror-Annual-2-WHA-ebook/dp/B076Z4T3YF/ref=asap_bc?ie=UTF8

www.ingramcontent.com/pod-product-compliance
Lightning Source LLC
Chambersburg PA
CBHW060826120626

46557CB00001B/394